Olive Jennie Bixby

My child-life in Burmah : or, Recollection and incidents

Olive Jennie Bixby

My child-life in Burmah : or, Recollection and incidents

ISBN/EAN: 9783337215774

Printed in Europe, USA, Canada, Australia, Japan

Cover: Foto ©Andreas Hilbeck / pixelio.de

More available books at **www.hansebooks.com**

MY EARLY HOME.

MY

CHILD-LIFE IN BURMAH;

OR,

Recollections and Incidents.

OLIVE JENNIE BIXBY.

BOSTON :
PUBLISHED BY W. G. CORTHELL,
MISSION ROOMS.
1880.

INTRODUCTION.

To the literature of Christian missions in foreign lands, there have been added of late frequent and excellent contributions. It is a cheering fact, that the number of those who read books treating of heathen communities, and of the labors, the struggles, and the achievements of the heroic men and women who have been and are now engaged in the noble work of propagating the gospel of Christ in unevangelized countries, is being rapidly multiplied. The geography, the topography, and the natural productions of the lands to which missionaries, in increasing numbers, are being sent from Christian countries ; the political governments, the social customs, the home life, the moral condition, the religious worship, and the spiritual destitution of the dominant nations and numerous subject tribes among whom missions are being planted, — are more extensively and far better known to-day than ever before. As a result, there is a more prevalent, intelligent, and fervid zeal among Christians in Christian lands, to enlighten and save the benighted and perishing millions of souls in

v

M629354

heathen lands. Let such books be multiplied and read, let such knowledge as they convey be more widely and rapidly disseminated in Christian churches and family circles at home, and we may confidently anticipate, as the outcome of an advancing acquaintance with missions, a more general, vigorous, and efficient prosecution of the grand work of the world's evangelization.

The manuscript of this unpretentious volume, now to be sent forth on its errand of instruction and usefulness, was placed in my hands by its author, with the request that I would examine it ; and, if upon examination I should think it worthy of publication, she would have me write for it an introduction. The manuscript I have read through with unabating interest ; and it gives me unfeigned pleasure to perform the slight service which has been asked of me.

The writer, who here tells the story of her childhood passed with her worthy missionary parents in Burmah, presents herself before the public in the capacity of an author, with very great hesitation. It is simple justice to say in her behalf, that she has found it difficult to overcome her reluctance to prepare this narrative for publication. She has braced herself to the task under appeals and encouragement from friends, who heard her read, at a woman's missionary meeting, a brief paper in which she simply attempted to give a few reminiscences of her early life among a heathen people. Those friends felt persuaded that, with such amplification as that paper was capable of receiving at her hands, she could make a book that was much needed, and might be eminently attractive and useful in Sunday schools and family circles. Thus prompted to extend her effort in that direction, and encouraged to hope that she might render some valuable service to the cause of missions, she proceeded to make a larger draft upon her memory, and to call up such scenes and incidents in her child-life in Burmah as are found described in the following pages. She has, we think, performed the task, undertaken at the solicitation of others, with admirable simplicity and directness. In a style unaffected and lucid, she presents simple facts, making no attempt to attain to the romantic and sensational, though that were easy and allowable with such materials as she had at her command. But she gives us a map instead of a painted landscape. Macaulay, contrasting two methods of writing history, remarks, " The picture, though it places the country before us, does not enable us to ascertain with accuracy the dimensions, the distances, and the angles." The map, he proceeds to say, " presents no scene to the imagination, but it gives us exact information as to the bearings of the various points, and is a more useful companion to the traveller or the general than the painted landscape could be." The author of this book on " MY CHILDHOOD " is evidently and supremely intent on presenting her readers with "exact information," aiming at verity, simplicity and

usefulness, rather than embellishment, picturesque-
ness, and fascination. But we venture to say that all
who shall begin to read this book will continue to
read to the close. It deserves, and we hope it will
have, a wide circulation.

W. S. McKENZIE,
District Secretary, A. B. M. U.

BOSTON, June 22, 1880.

PREFACE.

On board the sailing ship " Ino," May, 1856, off the coast of the Cape of Good Hope, a missionary was walking the floor of his cabin, carrying in his arms the tiny, wasted form of his infant child ; while in the berth near by lay the fond, suffering mother, unable to minister to the simplest wants of her babe. Deprived of all natural nutriment, and sustained only by the sweetened, soft-boiled rice, prepared by the father's hand, the life of the sick child hung by a very slender thread. The mother's feet were even now bathed in the first rippling waters of the river of death ; but, looking up into the face of him who was almost crushed by his weight of woe, she said, "I shall die, but little Jennie will live to be a solace to her father when I am gone."

From my earliest recollection an intense desire has possessed my soul to consecrate the life, so wonderfully spared, to the work of leading to Jesus the destitute millions in the land of my birth. And if through the following pages any are led to devote themselves, their means, or their prayers, to this glorious cause, I shall be amply repaid.

THE AUTHOR.

PROVIDENCE, R.I., June 22, 1880.

CONTENTS.

xi

CHAPTER VII.

CHAPTER VIII.

CHAPTER IX.

CHAPTER X.

CHAPTER XI.

CHAPTER XII.

MY

CHILD-LIFE IN BURMAH.

CHAPTER I.

BURMAH, FIRST IMPRESSIONS. — STAY IN RANGOON. — UP
THE TOUNGOO RIVER.

THE Burman Empire lies between the
Salwen River on the east and the Brah-
mapootra on the north-west and north; while
its western and southern shores are washed
by the Bay of Bengal, which separates it from
the peninsula of Hindostan.

Besides the noble rivers which form its
boundaries, its entire length from north to
south is traversed by the Irrawaddy, which,
after a course of twelve hundred miles, empties
by many mouths into the Bay of Bengal.
Rangoon, the chief seaport of Burmah, is situated on one of the mouths of this river, and
has a fine harbor.

13

Imagine yourself on board a British steam-ship, slowly making its way into the harbor of Rangoon.

It is one of the perfect days so well known in the tropics. There is a softness entirely new to you in the breezes that come from the shore, laden with the breath of flowers and the odors of sweet spices. There is a profounder depth to the fathomless blue above, and a fairer tint to the fleeting clouds, than you are accustomed to see in our dear New England. Land, which a few hours ago presented itself in dusky line along the horizon, is now clearly visible. An extensive plain lies before you, presenting the varied beauties of a tropical landscape. As you approach the city, little boats come out, bringing mangos, cocoanuts, plantains, and other fruits for sale. You see a confused mass of trees, houses, and pagodas, rising, apparently, to the clouds; but gradually confusion gives way to order. You see distinctly the great Shway-da-Gōng pagoda, whose gilded "*H'tee*," or umbrella-top, glistens in the sunshine. You hear a grating sound: it is the anchor thrown overboard, and the cable paid out. The noble ship that has been your home for forty days rests. You clamber down the sides into the ship's boat, or native *sampan*, waiting to receive you. A few strokes of the oars by the half-naked, brawny boatman, and you are clambering up the wet and slippery steps of the "*t'dah*," or wharf. You hear the hum and noise of a busy city; you are surrounded by dusky faces, and 'bewildered by strange sights and sounds.

It was thus that my father and my mother found the long journey with its perplexing changes over, and themselves on Burmah's shore. I was then five years old, and looking for the first time consciously upon my native land.

The ever open door of the hospitable missionary received us to its friendly shelter.

Toward evening the day after our arrival, my father and mother, taking me with them, drove out to a neighboring village to secure for a teacher a man who had been recommended to them as speaking several languages. We found him surrounded by a group of natives, a marked man among them. Lithe of figure, with a brilliant black eye and intelligent face, he seemed just the one they wanted. He promised to come the next day; and, true to his word, he arrived before six o'clock in the morning. It was interesting to see his awe and wonder as he entered the Christian home, so different from his own. He could hardly return the salutations, but sank upon his heels in the centre of the room, and thrusting his cigar into the lobe of one ear, — a beautiful orchid ornamented the other, — he gazed about the room. Arrangements were completed, and he became my parents' teacher in the Shan language during their month's stay in Rangoon.

Our home was to be in Toungoo, about two hundred miles, by the river, north of Rangoon. When the time for our departure arrived, Moung Saing, the teacher, wished very much to accompany us ; but his wife was unwilling to go. If he left her she would be free, according to Shan custom, to marry whomsoever she chose. He was ready to risk that, but of course my father would not allow it. Not long after, she died, and he came to us in Toungoo. The second day after his arrival, he came to the house early in the morning, his black eyes twinkling, and his face all aglow. Sitting down on the floor directly in front of my father, he began to talk rapidly and earnestly. The substance of his communication was this : He had met among our people, the day before, a Shan woman, who, with her father, had just arrived from the Shan States. He said she was beautiful and interesting, and willing to marry him ; and, if the teacher did not forbid, he would take her for his wife. The teacher asked if he was sufficiently acquainted with her. "Oh, yes ! very well acquainted," he said : "he had talked with her the evening before."

It was not exactly in accordance with the Christian view of the acquaintance that should precede a marriage that is to be a sacred, lasting obligation ; but it was native heathen custom, and nothing better could be expected of them. They were married by eating rice together, and remained with us as long as I staid in the country.

While in Rangoon we received a visit from Mah Men Tha, who was my nurse during the first three months of my life, for I was born in Maulmain during my father's first residence in the country. My nurse was very glad to see her "*mengalay*," or little girl. She then had a nice family of children, and was bringing them up in the fear of the Lord.

At the end of a month my father had completed his arrangements for going up the river. He had hired a native boat, stored it with pro-

visions for twenty days, and loaded it with supplies for future use in Toungoo.   It had no bed,
chair, or table ; but, having spread some clean
mats on the bottom, we took possession of it for
the journey.   How can I give an idea of this
floating-habitation?   The Burmans estimate the
size of boats by the number of baskets of
paddy, or unhusked rice, which they will hold.
A boat that would contain three hundred baskets of paddy answered our purpose.   It was
about thirty feet long.   The helmsman occupied a high chair in the stern, while at his feet
a little coop covered with thatch served as a
shelter for us.   A large barrel tipped over on
one side, and open at either end, would resem-
ble it in shape.   A little in front was a place,
emphatically *sitting-room*, for the thatch roof
was so low that no grown person could stand
erect.   Our seats were lockers on either side ;
a board placed from end to end was our table.
In this elegant style we passed a little more
than three weeks.   The boatmen with their
oars and poles and chatties and rice occupied
the front of the boat.   Rowing when the tide
was favorable, poling when there was no tide,
catching at the stout grass and bushes on the
bank when some quick, sharp eddy would carry

A RIVER IN BURMAH.

us down, we made our slow, monotonous way
up to our future home. The banks of the
river were diversified with impenetrable jungle,
groves of tall trees, patches of cultivated lands,
and here and there a village, a priest's *khy-oung*, and a pagoda. Most of the pagodas were
old, some in ruins ; one in particular was over-grown quite to the summit with grass, weeds,
and flowers. Along the banks, as the tide re-ceded, we saw the tracks of numerous croco-diles ; and in the eddies, or little pools which
the waters left, were many little fish cut off from
retreat, which the tall white rice-bird, the bril-liant flamingo, and the pouch-billed pelican
eagerly devoured, or carried away for their
young.

Sometimes a huge crocodile would be seen
basking in the sun. What man or boy, with a
gun in the boat, could resist the impulse to fire
at him ? The surprised creature with a sudden
plunge would disappear, but we soon saw him
again floating as calmly as if nothing had trans-pired.

Monkeys grinned and chattered in the trees,
sometimes following us along the banks, making
what might seem, with a little stretch of the
imagination on the Darwin side, frantic efforts

for the recognition of their cousins in the boat. Indeed, as I recall the scene, the monkeys, the natives, and the missionaries, I am half inclined to ask, Are we evolved? But there is this fact for answer: the monkeys are monkeys still; they grin no more gracefully, they chatter no more grammatically, than they did ages ago. The natives, some of them, are changed. Instead of wallowing stolid and half-nude in the mud, they are sitting clothed and in their right minds. They have been evolved from the depths and darkness of heathenism into the light of the knowledge of God.

The solitary palm-tree, giving name to the village of Tantabin, and the steep banks of the river, showing that we were near Toungoo, were a welcome sight. As we approached the landing, we saw the venerable Dr. Mason walking up and down the bank with his step-daughter, Miss Helen Bullard, waiting our arrival. The sight of those bright Christian faces in the midst of heathenism was like a gleam of sunshine to our hearts.

CHAPTER II.

HOME OF MY CHILDHOOD. — THE BAZAAR. — PAGODA. — OUR
FIRST HOUSE. — EARLY CONVERTS.

WE were now in Toungoo, a city dear to the
Burmans as the ancient capital of the empire,
their pride as a populous, thrifty city, their joy
as a centre for peaceful homes. To the English
it was an important military station, the last
taken by them from the Burman king: it was
also a centre of trade, consisting largely in timber, earth-oil, salt, rice, and lacquer-work. To
the missionary it was a hot-bed of heathenism,
the city and district containing hundreds of
thousands who had never heard the gospel. It
was, nevertheless, a hopeful field. Refreshing
dews of heavenly grace had already fallen on
the parched and thirsty ground, and showers of
mercy were yet in store. It was to *me* my
childhood's home, beautiful Toungoo. Never
to be forgotten are the emotions and experiences
associated with it. Its picture is clear upon
memory's tablet. Standing on the river's bank

not far from our home, and looking eastward, the turbid current of the Sitang River rolls at your feet. Beyond it is an interval of open, cultivated land, Burman and Karen villages, dense jungles, tall forests, and lofty mountains ; and spread over all — sometimes like a filmy gauze, sometimes like burnished gold, and some-times a clear ethereal blue — is the eastern sky.

Turning to the west, a little streak of civili-zation — the English department — lies before you, separated by a moat from the crumbling walls of the pagan city.[1] Crossing the moat by the principal thoroughfare, you enter the city's crowded streets, and soon come to the busy ba-zaar. At the entrance you notice the "tables," with little piles of rupees and other coins upon them, and "the money-changers sitting." Pass-ing along through numerous stalls, you will find in one a turbaned Mohammedan selling bright-colored handkerchiefs. In another, a wide-trousered Hindoo ready to serve you with mus-lins, calicoes, and white cloth : the larger the number of yards you buy, the higher the price he wishes per yard. In other places are Bur-

---

[1] This moat was formerly easily filled with water. It is now dry, and in many places filled up, and cultivated with vegetables and flowers.

man women with trays of jack-fruit, plantains, oranges, and cigars ; Shans with beautiful lacquer boxes, and coolies with odorous "*nga-pee*." [1] Here and there sits a Persian, calmly smoking his fragrant hookah. Timid Karens, black, white, and red,[2] flit back and forth, making purchases for their mountain homes. The brisk Chinaman, the sauntering English soldier, the proud Jew, old and young, boys and girls, meet and mingle, buy and sell, barter and get gain. You hear a jargon of voices that makes you think of the Tower of Babel ; you see sights from which you instinctively turn away ; and you inhale odors that send you in haste, and half breathless, into the outer and open air.

Leaving the bazaar, and passing through the city by the principal street, which the English government has made a pleasant drive, you come to the old palace-ground, a beautiful level greensward. Not a vestige of its former grandeur remains. Tall century-palms are growing from the ruins of its old wall, and native huts are crowding into its sacred precincts. Near this

[1] Fish are spread upon mats, and exposed to the sun for several days. They are then gathered up, and spices put in to arrest the decomposition. It is then potted, and kept for use.

[2] So called on account of the prevailing color of their dress.

ground is a somewhat remarkable pagoda. It is
called Shway-san-daw, or the Pagoda of the
Golden Hair, because it is said that three of
Gaudama's hairs were laid beneath its founda-
tions. Near the pagoda, as usual, is the idol-
house. The principal idol in this is a reclining
image of their dead and annihilated god, Gaudama. Smaller images in sitting posture, made
of marble, bronze metal, brick or wood, gilded
or ungilded, are placed in niches or on shelves
around the walls. There are often thank-offer-
ings from persons who have received special
blessings, as they suppose, in answer to their
prayers. Before the image are placed little
wooden candlesticks, holding very small candles
which are sometimes lighted; and small carved
pedestals to which are fixed strips of paper on
which a prayer is written, and thus continually
offered, bringing great merit to the suppliant.
Sometimes bamboo sticks, split at one end and
driven into the ground at the other, hold these
continually offered prayers; but, the costlier the
gift, the greater the blessing. Before all these
are placed clean mats, on which men and boys
kneel, or prostrate themselves, to say their
prayers. Farther removed and lower down,
trampled over by careless feet, is the place for

the women and girls in their devotions. Their touch would pollute the higher platform; but here they may humbly worship their partial god. A wooden shelf is placed on bamboo sticks near by, as an altar to receive the offerings of rice, plantains, and hard-boiled eggs, which crows and dogs speedily devour; but it makes no difference to the devotee: he obtains merit, whatever becomes of his offering. The inhabitants of the town and villages around come often in great numbers to this pagoda, to bring their gifts, and say their prayers. They have no sabbath, but every eighth day from the new moon is a worship-day, and special offerings are carried to the pagoda. Sometimes a fit of devotion seizes some man who wishes special merit, or hopes to become a god; and, taking a little silver gong, he goes through the city every evening before sunset, beating his gong, and calling in a sing-song tone for the people to come and worship at the pagoda. He soon has a train of followers, increasing as he proceeds, chiefly of women and children, bearing bright flowers, parched rice, and paper prayers, to leave at the sacred shrine. *They worship with their substance:* when shall all Christians learn to honor God with theirs?

Returning to the bazaar, we find near it our chapel, the only one in all that city devoted to the worship of the true God. Around it cluster precious memories. Not far from it is a Catholic church, a Mohammedan mosque, a Jewish synagogue, and an elegant Brahmin temple. All forms of Paganism and all kinds of sin are found in these Eastern cities. The missionary dwells here, as did the church in Pergamos, "even where Satan's seat is."

In Dr. Mason's hospitable house we made our home for three or four weeks, until my father succeeded in obtaining a house for himself. This was no easy matter, for "a tenement to let" is not often found in a native town. At last he secured a house situated in cantonment, and once occupied by an English officer. It was in a dilapidated condition, the roof being almost entirely gone, and the walls falling to pieces. As this was the rainy season, a roof was indispensable. The natives soon constructed one of thatch, and, platting wide strips of bamboo for the walls, tied them to the upright posts, and our house was ready. It fronted the parade-ground, which was a source of great pleasure to me; for, as Toungoo was under the Queen's protection, part of a British regiment was sta-

tioned there, and used the ground for their drills
and dress-parades. Occasionally the band played
there for an hour in the evening.

A short time before our arrival, several thousand Shans had taken refuge in British Burmah
from oppressive Burman taxation, and had settled about seven miles from Toungoo. For
incidents connected with our work among them,
see the book entitled "Our Gold-Mine," written
by Mrs. Ada C. Chaplin.

The first convert to Christianity was a Burman
woman, baptized in 1861. Others soon followed,
notwithstanding bitter persecution. The case
of Moung O was particularly interesting to me.
He was employed in the care of our ponies, but
spent much of his leisure time in reading the
Bible. God's word is quick and powerful, and
he soon accepted it as the guide of his life.
One day, while he was leading my pony, I asked
him, "Moung O, do you love Jesus?" He
quickly answered, "*Hoke, mengalay*" ("Yes,
little one "). "Then, why are you not baptized,
as Jesus commands?"— "Ah!" he said, "if I
confess Christ, my friends will all persecute me."
Not long after, he took up his cross, and followed
Jesus into the watery grave. Immediately the
storm of persecution which he foresaw burst

upon him. His wife refused to live with him, and his friends forsook him. I remember well the evening when he came from his house with a little bundle under his arm ; and, sitting down our steps, he said, " Teacher, I have no friends now : I have come to live with you. I love my wife, but *I love Jesus more.*" He began immediately to prepare himself to preach. It was not long before his wife returned to him, and, after much urging, consented to live on our premises ; still she avoided all religious influence. After a while, at the hour of our evening Burman worship she would sit on the steps outside, where she could hear the singing. Soon she came to the doorway, and one evening crept inside. It was not long before she joined the praying band, and for years the two were faithful laborers for the Master. Both have since died in the faith.

CHAPTER III.

THE NEW HOUSE. — REPTILES AND INSECTS. — THE CEN-
TURY-PALM. — FRUIT-TREES. — THE BANIAN. — FLOWER-
ING AND MEDICINAL PLANTS. — CULTIVATION OF RICE.

WHEN I was about eight years old, my father
built a house for the mission on a lot opposite
the main entrance to the city, where four principal streets met. It was a most favorable location for access to the people. The house was
built mainly of plain teak boards, and resem-
bled, on the inside, a country barn, with beams
and rafters in plain view. To secure the free
circulation of air, the house was raised upon
posts so high that a carriage could drive under
it, and from its piazza I have stepped upon the
back of an elephant. The building of a house
in Burmah is a very different affair from what
it is here. The first thing to be done is to send
to the forests for timber. Two kinds of timber
are chiefly used in building, — teak and ironwood. Teak is prized for its durability, delicacy
of fibre, and beauty of finish, in which respect

it greatly resembles mahogany. It is also proof
against white ants, who delight to devour almost
every thing else. Ironwood, as its name implies,
is valuable for hardness and durability. Natives
are very careless of the forests, and would cut
down any and every tree as their present interest or caprice might dictate; but the English
government has an interest in preserving these
valuable woods, and they are watched over by
persons called, as in England, foresters. The
trees being selected, they are cut down by natives, not with axes, for they have none, but with
"*dahs*," or large knives. The branches are cut
off, and the trunks are dragged by elephants to
the river, whence they are floated down to a convenient place near the town. Here a pit is dug,
across which the logs to be sawed into boards
are placed. Two men taking a long saw with
a handle at each end, and standing one in the
pit and one on the log above, slowly and labori-
ously accomplish the work of sawing. The
ironwood trunks that are to be the posts of the
house are taken to the spot selected for building.
Then follows the raising, which reminds one of
the old times in New England. Forty or fifty
men are gathered together. First, with narrow
spades about two inches in width, they dig holes

in the earth four or five feet deep and about ten feet apart. Into these holes the solid trunks of the trees are placed, and made to stand upright. These vary in length from fifteen to thirty feet, the shortest supporting the floor and the longest the roof. Great excitement prevails when these are set up ; as they have no machinery but ropes, bamboos, and their brawny hands. When these posts are placed, and fixed by means of cross-pieces nailed to them, the " raising " is done, and then follows the feast. A bushel of rice has been boiled without salt, and a condiment (or curry) made to eat with it, consisting of a little beef or fish, a great deal of red pepper, a plenty of some vegetable oil, and a variety of aromatic seeds carefully rubbed into a paste between two stones. A washbowl-full of rice and a cup of curry are taken out for the head man, or master workman, who eats by himself ; and the rest is poured into large trays, around which all indiscriminately " fall to," and, without knives or spoons, soon leave nothing but the trays remaining. Unfortunate is the one who eats longest, as he must wash the tray. After this, a basket of bananas or pine-apples and cigars completes the festival, and the satisfied, careless coolies saunter home. The carpenter then takes up the work, and with a "*dah*," hammer, and chisel, for his box of tools, slowly con- structs a habitation which, when occupied by a Christian family, has in it all the elements of home.

Sometimes a post will be too long.   The car- penter carefully measures the amount to be cut off, and then, lest he should remove too much, takes about half of it for his first cutting.   With hammer and chisel, bit by bit he cuts off this portion, and then measures again.   Of course it is still too long, and in the same way he re- moves another portion ; sometimes he makes a third cutting before it is right.   It is for his interest not to get the work done too soon, as he is paid twenty-five cents a day, and it may be a long time before he builds another house for a white man.

You must not think our Burman home was utterly devoid of beauty.   It was in a land

> " Where every prospect pleases,
> And only man is vile."

In front of the house was a garden full of bril- liant, sweet-scented flowers ; and among them many of my childish hours were spent.   There was a large red flower with which I used to

black my slippers. Rubbing the flower on the
slipper imparted to it all the shine one could
wish. Back of the house stood a large cluster
of bamboos, which is connected in my mind
with a snake adventure. Two large snakes
took refuge in the bamboos one day. After the
natives had killed the first one, they climbed
up, spear in hand, until within reach of the
other. When ready to strike at him, he disap-
peared among the leaves, and soon thrust his
head out far above them, and looked down with
a wise, saucy look, as if to say, " Did you catch
me ?" This he repeated again and again. After a long struggle they killed him ; and, having
exhibited him in triumph, some of the natives
carried him away to eat.

For a long time after moving there, daily war
was waged with snakes. The place had been
neglected, and the thick grass afforded them a
nice home. A nest of cobra's eggs was found
one day, and destroyed with great celerity.

Reptiles and insects, though numerous, never
caused us much serious injury. We were constantly on our guard, however. At night our
stockings must be carefully put away lest the
rats carry them off, and every article of clothing
must be examined before dressing in the morn-

ing, lest some poisonous visitor be concealed therein. Ten little scorpions were found one day snugly ensconced in my father's hat. A little red centipede slept under my pillow one night. Beautiful lizards constantly ornamented our walks, darting hither and thither in pursuit of flies and moths which constitute their food. It was no unusual thing for one to fall from the ceiling upon our table, as we sat at dinner or tea, sometimes breaking off his tail by the fall. When that happened, the astonished little creature would turn, look sadly upon his severed, wriggling member, and then dart away. One, at least, of a large species of lizard always dwelt in the rafters and eaves, whence his loud and solemn voice frequently startled us. The native girls used to tell fortunes by the utterances of this lizard. When he called out *toukteh*, they said, "city chap;" *toukteh* again, "country fellow;" and so they alternated till the animal wound up with *teh-teh-teh*. The appellation last used with his call would be that, as they thought, of their future betrothed. Pretty little birds called *mynahs* built their nests in the eaves of the house, and these large, ugly *touktehs* ate their eggs. They also infested dovecotes, sometimes quite breaking up the homes of the beautiful birds.

The little white ant, or termite, was a formidable foe to the comfort of our daily life. The
earth everywhere seems to be full of them.
They are most voracious little creatures : nothing but teakwood, metals, and earth-oil seems to
"come amiss" with them. All bureaus, trunks,
and boxes containing books or clothing must be
raised from the floor on bricks or teak blocks,
and frequently examined, or, ere you are aware,
their contents are riddled by these little pests.
Although so destructive to things immediately
before your eyes, they are seldom seen, as they
work always in the dark. They build for themselves a covered way from their nests in the
ground to the article they propose to devour.
The careful housekeeper often interrupts their
designs by discovering a little line of mud across
the floor, or up a post, or along the ceiling.
This is their covered road ; and with broom and
boiling water, and no small degree of impatience,
she puts an end to their advances in that direction. The natives, once a year, take a grand
revenge for their depredations. They eat them.
When the rains have fallen, and softened the
earth, a part of the white ants take wings, and
for one short night disport themselves in the
open air. They begin to come out of the earth

at about sunset, and the air until dark seems to
be full of them. Like other insects flying in
the night, they are attracted to light. The natives spread mats, place upon them basins of
water and a light. The unsuspecting ants fly
through the light, singe their wings, and fall
into the water, whence they are taken by the
delighted natives, and fried for the next morning's breakfast.

A variety of fruit-trees grew around the house.
In one corner of the compound there was an
old well, around which clustered several banana-
trees, and towering above them all stood a grand
old century-palm. Very beautiful was this tree
in its hundredth year, crowned with its pyramid
of white flowers, which soon ripened into fruit.
Then its work was done; its life was lived. It
had spent a hundred years in growth. It had
consumed a hundred years of rain and sunshine
for one short year of flowers and fruit. The
first wind that followed the perfected fruit laid
the lofty centenarian low. It had shown no
signs of decay. We only knew its end was
near by the perfection of its beauty and utility.
What scenes had this palm-tree witnessed in its
hundred years ? A king proudly strode by, when
with his own hand he could have torn it from

the soil. He had lived and reigned and died;
his palace had crumbled into dust, and other
palm-trees were growing where he had "eaten
rice." Idols of different nations had been carried in gay procession beneath its fan-like leaves;
priests had rested and cooled themselves in its
shade, and had been carried past it to their final
burning. Warriors and boatmen, coolies and
children, had fought and wandered, worshipped
and played, grown old and died, while it was
slowly growing, counting its years by each circle
of leaves that drooped and dried, above which
the towering top was always green, and beneath
which the stalwart trunk was never bowed. At
the commencement of its last decade there was
mingled with the rustle of its leaves the sound
of the English fife and drum, harbinger of re-
treating Burmese dominion, waning Buddhism,
religious liberty, and Christian triumph. Ere
the trees that are now springing from its ripened
seed shall bear their fruit, and die, the

> "Boodh shall fall, and Burmah's sons
> Shall own Messiah's sway."

Other parts of the compound [1] were occupied

---

[1] The compound, in India and Burmah, is the enclosure containing the dwelling, other houses, and gardens. It varies in
size from two or three to eight or ten acres.

by houses for native preachers and teachers, and the Shan schoolhouse. Not far from the house was the river ; and on the other side, in the distance, rose range after range of hills and mountains.

The fruit-trees of Burmah are numerous, and fruit forms a considerable part of the food of the natives. The mangosteen is one of the most delicious of fruits, but not very widely spread. The dorian is regarded by the natives as second to none, and the King of Burmah requires a tax of many hundreds annually to be contributed to the royal table. It has this peculiarity : to those who like it, it is most delicious ; to those who do not like it, it is most disgusting. The mango is a general favorite, rich and juicy. It is often compared to the peach, but is far more delicious in flavor and delightful to the taste. The fruit on the table for dessert the day of our arrival in Burmah was the pawpaw, or papaya. It somewhat resembles a melon in shape ; but its pulp is golden and fragrant, and its small black seeds have a peppery taste. It also grows in our own Southern States. Several guava-trees grew in front of our house ; and their white fruit, resembling in shape our small pear, afforded me much pleasure. There

was also the custard apple, in size and taste
resembling a rich cup-custard, but in outward
appearance more like a huge green raspberry.
The pine-apple is very abundant, and needs no
description. The plantain, or banana, is as
much prized there as the apple is with us.
There are as many as twenty-five varieties.
Some kinds are eaten as fruit ; others are very
nice fried or roasted, and eaten as a vegetable.
Orange-trees are abundant and prolific. A tree
planted by Dr. Mason produced, in its ninth
year, more than two thousand oranges. Sweet
limes resembling oranges, the small acid lime,
and the citron, or large acid lime, are found
almost everywhere. The mulberry-tree is cultivated extensively where the silkworm is raised.
The jujube, from which the famous jujube loz-
enges are made, is a small sour berry of which
the natives are very fond. The locust-trees,
which grow in many parts of America, sometimes remind one of the tamarinds in Burmah,
though the tamarind is larger, handsomer, and
has yellowish instead of white blossoms. It is
very valuable for its acid fruits used in curries.
It is not indigenous, but grows well with care.
The jack-fruit is very abundant. The tree is
large, and affords a dark, grateful shade. The

fruit, large as watermelons, grows from the trunk and large branches : obviously the small branches could not hold them. The bread-fruit, which sometimes has served missionaries for breakfast instead of bread, grows in the southern parts ; and the tapioca, whose root roasted resembles potatoes, grows in the mountains.

The most remarkable, in appearance, of forest trees is the banian. Its trunk sends out branches horizontally, which at intervals drop down shoots that descend to the ground, take root, and become trunks themselves ; thus spreading till one tree has become a large grove, and, as our geographies say, a thousand men may rest beneath its shade. This tree often nourishes itself at the expense of other trees. Its winged seeds find lodgement in the axils of the leaves of the palm-tree, and, moistened by the rains, send out rootlets that wind around the trunk of the palm, in and out among its old axils, till they take root in the earth. These rootlets grow till they seem like the folds of some huge serpent embracing the noble palm, gradually crushing out its life and consuming its body till there is finally no palm-tree there. A converted Burman who was one day talking with my father to a group of native people used this to illustrate the nature of little sins. He said, "A little banian-seed said to a palm-tree, 'I am weary of being tossed about by the wind : let me stay a while among your leaves.' — 'Oh, yes !' said the palm-tree : 'stay as long as you like,' and by and by forgot the little seed was there. But the seed was not idle. It sent out little fibres and tiny roots, and they crept around the trunk and under the bark and into the heart of the tree itself; and then the tree cried out, 'What is this ?' And the banian said, 'It is only the little seed you allowed to rest among your leaves.' — 'Leave me now,' said the palm-tree : 'you have grown too large and strong.' — 'I cannot leave you now : we have grown to-gether. I should kill you if I tore myself away.' The palm-tree bowed its head, and tried to shake the banian off, but could not; and, little by little, the palm-leaves withered, the trunk shrivelled, and only the banian could be found. Beware of little sins."

Of the many flowering trees of Burmah, the Amherstia is one of the most remarkable. The English gentleman who discovered it says, "There can be no doubt that this tree when in full foliage and blossom is the most strikingly superb object which can possibly be imagined."

The mesua is a favorite with the priests, and is planted around their monasteries. The Burmese say that their next Buddha, Aree-ma-daya, will enter the divine life while musing beneath its shade. The lofty champac shades the streets of towns and villages ; and its rich, fragrant blossoms are used by Burmese maidens to adorn their "long, dark hair." The delicate, sweet-scented blossoms of the mimusops are also prized for the same purpose. I have spent many a happy hour with the schoolgirls in stringing them upon a thread, and twining them about my hair. The gorgeous rhododendron delights us on every hand. Under the beautiful jonesia, it is claimed, Gaudama was born. "At the instant of his birth," say the sacred writers, "he walked seven steps ; and, with a voice like the roaring of the king of lions, he exclaimed, ' I am the most excellent of men, I am the most famous of men, I am the most victorious of men.' "

There is a species of butea which the Pwo Karens plant in their sacred groves ; and the deep, rich, orange blossoms, seen under a tropic sun in the dry season, present the appearance of a burning jungle. The henna-tree is extensively cultivated. The fresh leaves beaten with catechu,

> "Imbue
> The fingers' ends with a bright roseate hue,
> So bright, that in the mirror's depths they seem
> Like tips of coral branches in the stream."

The various species of jasmine, the trumpet-flower, the clerodendron, chaste-tree, and passion-flower are all prized for fragrance and beauty. One of the prettiest annuals is a species of sonerilla, with bright purple flowers. "The tuberose with her silver light" is extensively cultivated. The flower has a delightful fragrance, and throws out its odors strongest at evening. White, red, and blue water lilies are abundant. Various species of amaranth abound, also the pretty four-o'clock and the balsam. Orchids, or air-plants, most of which grow on trees, flourish everywhere, and the blossoms are surprisingly beautiful. Nearly every species is worth more in England than its freight over land, and they are often exported. Of one beautiful species the Karens are required to send several thousand annually as tribute to the king of Burmah.

Ferns are very interesting and numerous.

From the number and quality of medicinal

plants found throughout the country, it would seem, that, if they were fully understood, provision would be found among them for all the ills that flesh is heir to. The camphor-plant grows everywhere with the luxuriance of a common weed. The nux vomica, from which strychnos is extracted, grows in the vicinity of Toungoo. Dried senna-leaves are constantly for sale in the bazaar. Indian squills, ipecacuanha, gum-arabic, tragacanth, and the Toungoo gentian grow freely. The castor-oil and croton-oil plants, and the wood-oil tree, are largely cultivated. It is said that tobacco was introduced from America; but my father found it growing in great quantities upon the mountains, among savage tribes who had never held communication with people in the plain. It was universally used among them.

Coriander, anise, and cardamom seeds, sassafras, aloes, cinnamon, cloves, allspice, nutmeg, and mace are found. Black and cayenne pepper, ginger, and betel-nut are articles of commerce.

A great variety of vegetables is cultivated by the natives, but those best for Europeans are scarce. Nearly every plant is used as food by the natives. Several species of yam are cultivated. A very inferior sweet-potato is abundant, and native children eat them as we do apples. Varieties of beans are found, also radishes, mustard, the brinjal or vegetable egg, the tomato, and the onion. Cucumbers are eaten in large quantities; but the natives prefer them when large, ripe, and yellow, and think us very wasteful and mistaken in choosing those that are green and tender. More important than all these is rice, upon which the natives chiefly subsist. Scarcity or plenitude depends upon this grain. If the rice-crop is good, there is plenty, and the people are happy. If it fails, there is famine and distress. There are many varieties, both of mountain and lowland rice; and they are of all colors, from ivory-white to coal-black. From the black rice the Karens make a kind of bread, which is to them what gingerbread is to us. There is also a glutinous rice, which was very convenient for us in journeys. Joints of bamboo are filled with a quantity unboiled, a little water is added, and the opening closed. It is then roasted, and, when done, far surpasses any cake I ever ate. Mountain-rice is planted in the dry ground about the month of April, and the early kinds are reaped in August. Lowland rice, on the

contrary, is in June sown broadcast upon the
flooded fields ; and the rice grows as the rain
increases, keeping its head just above the water.
If the water overflows the rice, the crop is
spoiled or greatly damaged.   When the rains
cease, and the water decreases, the rice begins
to ripen ; and by November, when the ground
is hardened, the fields are ready for the reapers.
They cut the grain with a small sickle, tie it in
bundles, and pile it on a smooth piece of ground,
previously prepared, with the heads in the centre.   In some places young people tread out
the rice : in others they use buffaloes ; and, as
the latter help themselves to a mouthful whenever they choose, one is reminded of the verse
in Scripture, "Thou shalt not muzzle the ox
when he treadeth out the corn."   The next
thing is to remove the husks.   This may be
done in several ways.   I most frequently saw
them use a large wooden mortar and pestle :
two and often three women would pound in the
same mortar, alternating their strokes with
mathematical precision.   In other cases the
pestle was moved by a foot-treadle.   The mother would often tie her baby to her back, and,
standing with one foot on the treadle, thereby
lift the pestle ; when she removed her foot, the

pestle would fall, the monotonous swinging of her body at the same time rocking her baby to sleep. The last thing is to winnow it. With large quantities they often build a scaffolding several feet high, mount a bamboo ladder with a basketful at a time, and pour it down upon mats spread on the ground. The wind blows away the husks, and the clear rice remains.

CHAPTER IV.

The Animals of Burmah.

As Burmah lies partly in the torrid and partly in the temperate zone, it comprises among its animals many that are peculiar to both zones; so that the missionary is constantly surprised, now with delight in beholding the familiar creatures of his native land, and now with wonder as he gazes upon some denizen of the heated earth.

It is ten o'clock in the morning. A missionary's child is sitting on the veranda, gazing, half dreamily, into the heated atmosphere, and listening to the quiet sounds that fill it with life. She hears a gentle cooing, and rises to feed her beautiful tame pigeons, not with oats or corn, but with the delicate white rice. Her speckled pet fowl hastens, with motherly cluck, to call her downy brood of white chicks to share the feast; and a train of ducks, with their "Quack, quack," and outstretched glossy necks, waddle up the narrow path to get at

AN ORIOLE NEST.

least a grain; "Ahn, ahn," from the jack-tree
close by, shows at least a half-dozen hungry crows ready for their share, but far more
eager to seize the tiny pat of butter the missionary mother is so carefully putting away, or
to pounce upon the bit of beef the cook has
laid upon the shelf by the door, while he takes
off his turban and white dress. There is a
chattering in the bamboo hedge; and the child
looks eagerly for the little green parrots, which
she can scarcely distinguish from the leaves.
She hears a scream, and, look! there is a kite,
or hawk, slowly sailing off with one of the
beautiful birds in its talons. She looks across
to the open lot yonder, and sees a group of buz-
zards lazily lifting their wings, and giving a few
heavy jumps about, as they tear in pieces the
dead cat or dog left there for these scavengers,
who ravenously devour it. In the marshy moat,
the tall heron stalks, the pelican, coot, and
water-hen hide. Twitterings and a gush of
song greet the child's ear; and she looks up to
see the golden orioles darting in and out the
long necks of their curious nests, hanging from
the sheltered side of the palm-tree in the garden, or the eaves of her own dwelling. She
scatters another handful of rice, and the hoopoe

with wavering crest, and the trustful mynah with her five little ones just fledged, hop almost at her feet in picking it up. She hears a loud trumpeting. If her mother catches the sound, she is instantly transported to her native country, and half fancies she hears the hoarse whistle of the incoming train. But the little girl knows it is the elephant over yonder, dragging logs from the river to the saw-pit, or piling them up with his flexile trunk as evenly and exactly as any man could do. I never tired of watching the elephants. The keen twinkle of their small eyes, the lazy flap of their broad ears, the measured lifting of their huge feet, the nervous quiver of their thick skin, and the restless, swaying, sniffing, touching, searching movement of the long trunk, filled me with wonder. They seemed to belong to some faraway, early period of the earth's history, left over and forgotten by the years as they glided by. I tried to take a ride upon one once ; but the see-sawing motion of the *howdah* made me nervous, and his loud trumpeting filled me with fear, so I quickly asked to be put down. My father was about to make a journey into the jungles, and the elephant he had procured was fastened with an iron chain to a palm-tree in our yard. He had remained with apparent content during the day, feeding upon the limbs of an Indian fig-tree near by, crunching, as if they had been sugar-cane, the branches three or four inches in circumference. But at night, when the natives had gone into town, and every thing was quiet, we heard the dragging of a chain, and said, "The elephant is loose." My father went to the door, but in the darkness could see nothing; and, as he heard no movement, he concluded we were mistaken, and came back. As soon as all was still again, we heard the chain, as before. My father went very softly to the door, and found the elephant just going out at the gate. Mother hastily took a pan of rice, which she thought would take him a considerable time to eat, and held it out to him : what was her surprise to see him put the end of his trunk into the pan, draw up its entire contents, and pour them as one mouthful into his capacious throat! My father, however, had picked up the end of the chain, and the elephant patiently allowed himself to be refastened to the tree. Later in the evening, his driver, returning, found him just outside the compound, apparently considering which way to go. He made no resistance as he was led back again, and this time fastened with so many turns and twists and ties, it was thought impossible for him to get away; but in the morning there was no elephant to be seen. After three days search, he was found quietly feeding in a jungle, a mile and a half away. My father decided, that, though he seemed the most gentle and docile of his race, he was far too independent, and skilful in picking ties, to be useful in a jungle trip; and the elephant was sent home. Wild elephants are numerous and dangerous in the jungles; and the catching and training of them is a source of excitement, danger, and profit to those who are daring enough to engage in it.

The tiger is the most formidable of the wild animals. In making jungle-trips, it is necessary, when threading the narrow paths, to keep close together by day, and to keep large fires by night, lest some stealthy prowler pounce upon man or pony before any one is aware of his approach.

Only six miles from the city stood a heathen monastery on the edge of a jungle. One night a tiger entered the open house, and carried off a priest: he repeated these visits until he had carried away six men. The natives then went

ELEPHANT-HUNTING.

out to hunt for him, and soon carried him in
triumph through the town.

The buffalo is *the* animal of Burmah, as the
camel is of Africa, and the llama of South
America. It differs from the American buffalo,
which is not a buffalo at all, but a bison, and also
from the African animal of the same name. It
is larger than the common ox, and more powerful in figure. It has a thick, dun-colored, almost
hairless skin, and huge wide-spreading horns of
the same color as the skin. Its milk is rich and
nutritious, and, dying of itself, its flesh is used
for food. The Burmans never kill it: the Karens
often do.

It is their habit to feed and work during the
night, or in the cool of the morning and evening. When the heat of day begins, they at once
seek the rivers or pools, and submerge themselves, leaving only their heads in view; or they
seek some marshy place, and burrow in the mud
until completely covered, thus protecting themselves from mosquitoes, flies, and the scorching
rays of the sun. The buffalo is managed by a
ring thrust through the nose, to which is attached
the rope, by which it is led about or driven as
with reins. In the hands of the natives, it has
something like the patience and docility of the

ox, but is utterly intractable by Europeans. Unlike any other animal, it possesses a special, inveterate, and undying hatred for white people, and will often attack them. His repugnance is so great that he cannot endure the odor of a white person. If one comes within sight of a drove, they will immediately arrange themselves in line, elevate their noses in the air, and sniff and snort with the most intense disgust depicted upon their faces. One day, as a missionary and I were riding on our ponies, we saw a drove of buffaloes coming down the road. One broke loose, and was rushing down the street at full speed, when, seeing us, he charged for us. The gentleman was a little in advance of me. Just as the buffalo lowered his head to toss horse and rider into the air, he so managed his pony that he reared, and the buffalo glided under his fore-feet. He was going too fast to stop, and rushed on.

It is most humiliating to a white person, if he wishes to take a trip in a buffalo-cart, to be obliged to steal round to the back of the cart, and carefully climb in, while the native driver endeavors to soothe and divert his sensitive span. I remember, with curious emotions, a night's trip taken in one of those buffalo-carts.

A BURMAN CART.

Mats were spread in the rude wooden-wheeled vehicle, some articles of baggage were stowed away, and then we tried to dispose ourselves in the remaining space, too small for three to lie down. With a child's happy faculty of adapting one's self to circumstances, I fell asleep, lulled by the monotonous creak of the huge wheels and the nasal trills and quavers of the driver's weird song. The night was warm : we did not advance as rapidly as was necessary in order to reach our destination in the cool of the morning, and the scorching rays of the sun found us with several miles still to traverse. The driver declared we must wait until night, as he dared not use his buffaloes in the heat of the day. My father, feeling obliged to hasten, insisted on pressing forward. After much grumbling on the driver's part, we proceeded ; but, whenever we passed a stream or little pool of water, he would run with a bamboo, dip up water, and pour it upon the backs of his buffalos, to enable them to endure the heat.

The zebu, or Indian ox, with the large hump on its shoulders, is employed in some parts of Burmah as the buffalo is in others.

A missionary lady, describing a three days' ride in a bullock-cart, says, "The respect and

admiration for Burman carts and bullocks with
which that ride inspired me, I do not think I
shall ever outgrow. Any other vehicle would
have been overturned and smashed to pieces at
a dozen different stages; and any other beast
would have grown restive, and broken loose
before the distance was half made. As for the
driver, no words of mine could do justice to his
equanimity of mind, as, squatted upon the
tongue of the cart, he punched with a long
bamboo first one bullock and then the other,
uttering at intervals a soul-inspiring groan."

My mother used to say the one luxury of the
country was its beautiful ponies; and yet they
were not so much a luxury as a necessity.
Smaller than the horse, more timid, less patient,
and less to be relied on, they were nevertheless admirably adapted to the saddle and jungle
travel. They were our pets at home and our
friends abroad. They were so cheap and easily
kept, we could each have one. My little brother's, " Minnie Gray," cost five dollars; the light
sorrel in which I delighted, ten dollars; my
mother's, twenty, and so on.[1] A short daily
ride was essential to health when at home; and

---

[1] Such were the prices then. They are much higher now,
and the cost of keeping them is greater.

in a country where there were no railroads,
coaches, or horse-cars, in fact, where there were
no roads at all, with the exception of boats and
elephants, ponies are the European's only means
of travel. The buffalo hates the pony as he
does the white man, thus making the pony more
the white man's friend.

I should make this chapter quite too long,
were I to describe the monkeys, bears, wild
dogs, jackals, leopards, wildcats, squirrels, rats,
mice, wild hogs, deer, and rhinoceros, or even
mention, more than I have done, the great variety of birds of brilliant plumage and sweet song,
the multitude of reptiles that crawl at your feet,
the swarms of insects that fly in the air, or the
finny tribe that swim in the waters. No one
here need search in vain for any thing that

"O'er bog or steep, through strait, rough, dense, or
    rare,
  With head, hands, wings, or feet pursues his way,
  And swims or sinks, or wades or creeps or flies."

No part of the globe is more abundant in
vegetable productions, or diffuse and prolific in
its animal kingdom. Here too, as in all other
parts of the world, man holds universal sway
over every living thing. There are none so

large, so strong, so fierce, so wild, but he is able to tame or conquer. When shall he be consciously, devoutly, lovingly, subject to the great Ruler, the Creator of all? It remains very greatly with us, the young people of America, to answer that question. Shall we give them the light?

CHAPTER V.

TRANSMIGRATION. — RELIGIOUS FESTIVITIES. — RACES AND
COSTUMES. — NATIONAL PECULIARITIES.

THE Burmans believe in the transmigration
of souls; i.e., when any living being dies, some
other being is born, and the soul of the dying
enters into the body of the living, and so passes
through another period of conscious existence.
There is a "*Kahn,*" or fate, that governs these
changes. When some soul is sufficiently ad-
vanced to become a man, if he is a wicked man,
his soul must go back again through the lower
orders of life, till, having borne penalties for
some of its sins, it is permitted to be a man
again. If he now leads a devout life, he may
hope, in the next stage of existence, to be a
nat, and finally to be annihilated; i.e., delivered
from this wearisome round of being.

Woman, as such, can have no hope even of
annihilation. The law is made so difficult for
her to keep, that she is forced to believe it most
likely she will sink at once to the world of woe.

If she should escape that by leading a most devout, benevolent, and self-denying life, by worshipping continually her husband, the priests and pagodas, she *may possibly*, in her next stage of existence, be—a man. No higher hope than this can ever enter a Buddhist woman's heart.

The social element enters largely into the religious observances of the Burmans, as it did into those of the Jews in their early history. They make annual festivals at sacred places, where they gather in great numbers, clad in their gayest attire, and with merry hearts spend several days in worship, feasting, and amusement. At such times they make costly offerings to the priests and the pagodas. The women gather up all their little savings for the year, and buy yellow silk robes for the priests. The men make or purchase idols with which to decorate the idol-houses; or obtain pieces of gold-leaf, which they plaster upon the idols or pagodas, one joining his piece to some other's, till the whole is covered. They give always of their best to their helpless idol.

About eight miles from our house, were the "Seven Pagodas," a sacred place where Gaudama is said to have scratched for his breakfast when he was a rooster. These pagodas were

built in honor of that event. There is a footprint cut in a flattened rock not far from our
house, said to be that of Gaudama; and the
next footprint is at these seven pagodas, — it
being but one step for him from the one place
to the other. The footprints are enormous, and
are covered with figures that may be hieroglyph-
ics. My father and mother took me with them
to these pagodas on one of these annual gather-
ings. They remained several days, distributing
tracts, and talking to the people. My childish
heart was greatly saddened by the sight of such
idolatry, and filled with a longing to lead these
poor, degraded ones to seek "the Way, the
Truth, and the Life." One woman had with
her two little girls about my age. She took
them with her before the idol, and, placing some
parched rice in their little hands, taught them
to place them before their faces, bow to the
image, and repeat their prayers. Where are
those little girls now? I sometimes ask. Oh, if
I could have led them to Jesus then!

The people were mainly Burmans; but Shans,
Karens, and Hindoos mingled with them. The
Burmans, in their gay "*p'tsos*" and white-muslin jackets, with their long black hair coiled on
top of their heads, and often encircled by a gay

silk turban, formed a striking contrast with the Shans in their loose blue pants, white jackets, and broad-brimmed straw hats; as also to the numerous tribes of Karens in their varied and fantastic attire, and to the swarthy Hindoos in their loose white robes and snowy turbans.

Heathen Burmese women wear a gay-colored "*t'maing*" of cotton or silk, lined with muslin, folded about the form, extending from the arm-pits to the ankles, and open in front, so that in walking the limbs are exposed. In full dress, a white-muslin jacket with long close sleeves is worn over the "*t'maing*." Among the laboring classes and many married women, the *t'maing* is fastened at the waist, and nothing else is worn. Their hair is very abundant, black, and glossy. They comb it smoothly, and form it into a graceful knot behind, frequently adding chap-lets of fragrant flowers. To increase their beauty, they rub on the face a delicate yellow powder. They adorn themselves with huge earrings, numerous and costly necklaces, gold chains, rings, bracelets, and anklets. Mission-aries always strive to teach the native Christians to dress modestly and without extravagance; accordingly in all our schools the girls wear the closed *loonghee* instead of the open *t'maing*.

CHRISTIAN KAREN GIRLS.

They also lay aside their expensive ornaments, and the teachers endeavor to lead them to seek the better "ornament of a meek and quiet spirit."

Burmese boys often do not wear any thing until they are eight or ten years of age, nor the girls until four or five years old, except gold and silver and other ornaments in profusion. The boy then dons his *p'tso*, or strip of gay cloth, and the girl her tiny *t'maing*. Poor little things! they have a hard time in learning to keep them on ; for they use no buttons or pins, but merely tuck in the corners with a peculiar twist. The little inexperienced girl starts to run with a playmate, when off drops her *t'maing;* but she only stops for a moment, picks it up, and runs along again, carrying it in her hand.

There are marked differences between the three principal nationalities now existing in Burmah, — the Burmans, Shans, and Karens. The Burmans are very intelligent, polished, haughty, and somewhat indolent. The Shans are equally intelligent, less proud, and more diligent. Like the Burmans, they are Buddhists. The Karens are by far the most docile and lovable. They have been crushed by oppressive Burman rule, and there is an element of sadness in their disposition. They are not Buddhists, but worship spirits, and seem more susceptible to the gospel. We cannot, therefore, compare and judge of the work of missionaries among these different peoples ; for we cannot understand the helps and hinderances they meet with in the peculiar characteristics of the people for whom they labor. If we estimate success by the amount of error removed, and the difficulties overcome, it will probably be seen that as much has been accomplished for the Burmans as for the Karens. A Burman is well read in all their religious and scientific theories. The Karen has no books but what missionaries give him : he knows nothing, but he very readily acquires knowledge. It was Dr. Judson, I think, who remarked that the Karen stood with his empty chattie, into which the missionary could freely pour the precious truths of salvation ; while the Burman held his chattie filled with odious earth-oil, which the missionary must induce him to throw away, and cleanse the chattie, before it could be filled with the water of life. After baptizing two Burman men, Dr. Judson said, 'I baptized one hundred Karens when I worked among them before their missionaries were sent out, and these two Burmans have cost me more than the whole of that hundred Karens." Dr. Mason writes, " The first Burman I baptized had his attention drawn to Christianity by a tract that fell into his hands; and he kept reading and thinking to himself for two years before he called on me; and we had to converse and discuss every point of the Christian system and every doctrine of Buddhism a whole year before he could fully accept the offer of a free salvation; but, from the time that that point was reached, there has been no more faltering. He *knows* whom he believes. The faith of a Burman is the faith of a man, welling up from the depths of his mental faculties; but the faith of a Karen is the faith of a child, with no deep roots in the understanding. The Karens are like the Samaritans, who, at the first hearing, 'with one accord gave heed unto those things which Philip spoke;' but the Burmans are like the Bereans, who 'searched the Scriptures daily, whether these things were so.' "

It is a striking fact that the Karens have traditions of the scattering of the nations, and beyond this, of the deluge, and then of the creation and fall of man, coinciding wonderfully with the statements of the Bible. The following stanzas, translated by the late Dr. Mason, clearly illustrate this fact : —

"Anciently God commanded, but Satan appeared bring-
ing destruction.
Formerly God commanded, but Satan appeared deceiving
unto death.
The woman E-u and the man Tha-nai pleased not the eye
of the dragon.
The persons of E-u and Tha-nai pleased not the mind of
the dragon.
The dragon looked on them, — the dragon beguiled the
woman and Tha-nai.
How is this said to have happened ?
The great dragon succeeded in deceiving — deceiving
unto death.
How do they say it was done ?
A yellow fruit took the great dragon, and gave to the
children of God ;
A white fruit took the great dragon, and gave to the
daughter and son of God ;
They transgressed the commands of God, and God turned
his face from them.
They transgressed the commands of God, and God turned
away from them.
They kept not all the words of God — were deceived,
deceived unto sickness.
They kept not all the law of God — were deceived,
deceived unto death."

The Karens believe that every object in nature has its spirit lord, and every man a guard-

ian spirit and many unseen foes; to all these they must make annual offerings to secure their blessings, and avert their wrath and the calamities which they inflict.

The Karens usually bury their dead; but sometimes, if circumstances require haste, burn them, and then a bone is taken from the ashes, often the backbone. When at leisure a feast is made, and the bone is buried. At the feast the bone is placed in the centre of a large booth, and around it are hung the articles belonging to the deceased. A torch is placed at the head, and another at the foot, to represent the morning and evening stars, which, they say, are spirits going to Hades with lights in their hands. Around the whole a procession marches, singing dirges. The following is a specimen :—

"Mother's daughter is proud of her beauty;
Father's son is proud of his beauty;
He calls a horse, a horse comes;
He calls an elephant, an elephant comes;
On the beautiful horse, with a small back,
He gallops away to the silver city.
O son of Hades, intensely we pity thee,
Panting with strong desire for the tree of life.

The jambu fruit, the jambu fruit
Hangs drooping o'er the lake,

Red jambu flowers, red jambu flowers,
  Hang drooping o'er the lake.
Should seeds of the tree of life still exist,
Then man wakes up from death in Hades.
O son of Hades! intensely we pity thee,
Panting with strong desire for the tree of life."

CHAPTER VI.

HEATHEN FUNERALS. — THE PRIESTHOOD. — BUDDHISM.

ONE of the saddest sights to be seen in Burmah is a heathen funeral; and there is scarcely
a day but that one or more passes through the
principal streets. The coffin, covered with tinsel and bright-colored paper, is placed upon a
fantastic-looking car, that is decorated in the
same way, and often has the addition of a large
peacock-plume in each corner. This is borne
upon men's shoulders, and is accompanied by a
band of native music (?). They stop frequently,
and go through with a kind of drill or dance;
and it often seems as if the car would topple
over, and the coffin be broken to pieces. In the
procession frequently appear eight or ten carts,
bearing offerings to priests, besides a great
number of women carrying loaded trays upon
their heads. Children are buried, but the
bodies of adults are usually burned. The place
for burning, in Toungoo, was three miles out
of the city.

I once attended the funeral of one of their priests. It was an occasion of great festivity. The body had been embalmed for more than a year. It was a hot, sultry day. There was not a cloud to shield from the scorching rays of the sun, nor a breath of air to refresh the panting devotees ; but, regardless of this, the eager throng was slowly wending its way through the dusty streets. Not a tear, nor an expression of real sorrow, was seen or heard among the joyous crowd ; but, in thé distance, we heard the groans and lamentations of the hired mourners. Mounting our ponies, we joined the procession. As we passed the pagodas and khoungs, we saw men, women, and children prostrate before the idols, muttering over their rosaries their "vain repetitions," such as, "There is nothing real, there is nothing eternal, all is trouble."

On arriving at the grounds, we found bamboo booths scattered here and there, where native confectionery and fruits were displayed to great advantage. In the centre of the field was a curious structure, about twenty feet in height, resembling a pagoda. It was made of bamboos and paper, and covered with tinsel and lace. On the top was a large "*H'tee*," or umbrella, its rim surrounded with little tinkling bells, and with long lace streamers, which, floating in the breeze, wafted prayers to Gaudama in behalf of the departed one. About ten feet from the ground, in the centre of the structure, was an enclosed platform, upon which the body, elegantly attired and surrounded by gaudy trappings, was eventually placed for the burning. Above and below, the structure was filled with combustible materials. On each side of the car upon which the body was carried, were long ropes, held on the one side by Shans, and on the other by Burmans. The Shans tried to pull it towards themselves, crying, "You shall not carry this priest away;" while the others, pulling in the opposite direction, replied, "We will, yes, we will." In this manner they spent the greater part of the forenoon. Finally they attached it by the ropes to several similar but less gorgeous structures, and a herald announced that the burning would take place at four in the afternoon. In the mean time, we examined the various objects of curiosity, visited the stands, telling the way of life to all who would listen. In one circle drums were beating, girls were dancing, and people were laughing and quarrelling, a medley of confusion. In another group we found the jugglers, the snake-charmers, and

fortune-tellers. At the appointed hour the people gathered round the lofty bier. Rockets,
made to represent cannons, with grotesque images seated upon them, were sent shooting
along the ropes into the car. It was soon after
set on fire by the nearest relative, and the body
of the priest speedily consumed, amid the shout-
ings of the people, the beating of the drums,
and the roaring of the flames. The several at-
tendant cars were burned ; and the jaded crowd
returned to their homes without a tender re-
membrance of the departed, or a thought of
the solemn future. They returned to live on
in their ignorance and superstition, unless some
ray of light from the Sun of righteousness
should find its way to their hearts, and shed a
radiance there.

Buddhist priests are usually a lazy class of
men who enter the priesthood for the sake of
an easy, comfortable life. They practise all
manner of wickedness under the cloak of sanc-
tity. The laws of their religion forbid them to
wear any covering upon their heads, or sandals
upon their feet, or even to carry an umbrella.
They must beg their food from door to door ;
their clothing must be made of rags ; they must
not touch money, nor look at a woman. If a

priest's own mother fall into the river, he must
not touch her to help her out, though he may
throw her a stick, or something she can lay
hold of. They are intensely devoted to some
of the forms of their religion ; but those requir-
ing personal privation, they pass lightly over.
They go about the streets every morning, it is
true, to collect their food for the day ; but the
best of every thing is given them. Their clothing, so far from being made of rags, is often of
the most costly material ; though, where they
are particular to carry out the letter of the law,
it is cut into small pieces, and then sewed
together. They often acquire large sums of
money by the sale of articles that are presented
to them ; and in some cases they then throw
off their yellow robes, allow their hair to grow,
and, as they say, "become men again." The
priesthood in Burmah is arranged into a regu-
lar hierarchy. The highest man, called a *rahan-
da*, is a kind of archbishop, who presides over
all other priests, and appoints the chiefs of the
monasteries. He resides at the imperial court,
where he is regarded one of the greatest men
in the kingdom. Below him are various ranks.
of priests, all supported by the so-called volun-
tary offerings of the people. Their power over

the people is almost unlimited. If a priest re-
fuses to receive the offerings of any one, that
person is immediately regarded as tabooed, and
calamity, disaster, and ruin stare him in the face.
The priests are worshipped in the same manner
as the pagodas and images of Gaudama.

"Buddhism in its moral precepts," says one
who had personal acquaintance with it, "is, perhaps, one of the best religions ever invented by
man; but *its basis is entirely false.* Instead of
a heavenly Father forgiving, and filial service
from a pure heart as the effect of love, it presents nothing to love, for its deity is dead;
nothing as the ultimate object of action but
self, and nothing for man's highest and holiest
ambition but annihilation. Their doctrine of
merit leaves no place for holiness, and destroys
gratitude either to God or man. It ministers
to pride; for the very fact of his being *now* a
man assures the Buddhist, that in former trans-
migrations he must have acquired incalculable
merit, or he would not now occupy so distin-
guished a place in the scale of being. Their
system of balancing evil with good reduces all
sin to a thing of little importance. 'If any man
sin,' in Burmah, his religion tells him of 'no
advocate with the Father,' to whom he may

bring a believing, penitent heart; but, instead, it tells him he may repeat a form of words, he may feed a priest, he may build a pagoda, he may carve an idol, and thus balance his iniquity with merit."

An intelligent Burman, talking with my mother, said that his sins were ·as broad and deep as the ocean; but his good deeds were the ship in which he sailed safely over.

If any man suffer, in Burmah, his religion points him to no place where "the wicked cease from troubling, and the weary are at rest," and where "God himself will wipe away all tears;" but it dictates proud submission to unalterable fate, and flatters him that his sufferings here may free him from torment in some future existence.

If any man die, in Burmah, his religion tells him of no Saviour who has "passed through the grave," and swallowed up death in victory; but it threatens degradation, perhaps into a soulless brute, or, at best, into a place of expiatory misery. In short, living or dying, the Burman may be said to be "without hope and without God in the world."

CHAPTER VII.

THE SEASONS. — GLIMPSES OF MISSIONARY OCCUPATIONS. — THE SCHOOL. — MOUNTAIN-TRAVEL. — STORY OF MOUNG ONG.

IN Burmah there are two seasons, the wet and the dry. About the 10th of May, showers commence, and increase in frequency, until late in June it rains daily. This continues until the middle of September. Heavy rains then cease, but showers continue until the middle of October. Even in the rainy season the sun shines a part of the day, and the rankest vegetation covers every thing.

To give a clearer glimpse at missionary life, let me recall a day or two which are samples of most of the days in the dry season, when missionaries are not absent on jungle-trips. As there are no schools for missionaries' children, and no associates for them but natives, I was necessarily the companion of my parents in their visits among the people, as well as in their work at home.

Missionaries rise early, — some at four, most at five o'clock, — and take immediately their "little breakfast," a slice of bread and cup of tea. We would then mount our ponies, and ride two or three miles to some neighboring village, thus reaching the people before they began their daily toil. Sometimes the presence of the little white child would be sufficient to draw the whole village together ; sometimes my father would sing to attract them, and sometimes a desire to know more of the strange religion of which they had heard a little would bring them together. Often a group of women would gather about my mother, more curious about the whiteness of her hand, the length of her fingers, and the number of her garments, than desirous to know the way of life. But with these for a text, and their curiosity for a line of argument, she would weave into her answers to their questions the principal points of the "old, old story," and leave them with thoughts of Jesus stirring in their dark minds.

Sometimes these rides were prolonged to a village, or group of villages, at a greater distance, and the day spent among them. Of one such day my mother writes : " Spent the day at a Burman and some Shan villages. At first we saw only young persons, and inquired if there were no old people in the village; whereupon the 'oldest inhabitant' was immediately sent for. He was an unusually intelligent old man, eighty years of age. His hair was white as snow, but his eye brilliant and sparkling, and his teeth unimpaired. When he came to the house where we were, he stopped at the thresh-old, and repeated his Burman prayer, 'Anneitsa, dokah, annatta, P'yah.'

"We were sitting in the upper part of the house, and to reach us he must climb a little ladder. As he stepped upon the ladder, he stopped, and repeated his prayer again, and then greeted us most cordially. I wanted to lead his mind to the truth, and tell him of Jesus; so I spoke to him of his great age, his white hair, and the fact that we must all die. 'Yes,' he said with great earnestness, 'there are three evils we must all endure, — sickness, old age, and death.' Two of these he had already expe-rienced, and now death was near. Though he prayed very much, he could not be delivered from this last evil, — his god could not deliver him. 'Do you know any god,' he asked, that can deliver from these evils?'—'Yes,' I told him: "my God can deliver from all these. He

is not like Gaudama, who was sick, who grew
old, and died when he was just your age ; for my
God is the Eternal, forever established, always
the same. He is never sick ; he cannot grow
old ; he can never die. He can and will deliver
all who trust in him from all the evils of this
world and the greater evils of the next.' I
tried to tell him it was sin that brought death
into the world, and separated us from God ; so
that it was right for God, though he had all
power, to let us suffer and die before he received
us again to himself. But his mind seemed to
grasp only the one truth, that my God could
not grow old, be sick, or die.

"Soon he heard the assistant talking with
some men down-stairs, and he said, 'I will go
down, and listen.' As soon as he had joined the
group, he repeated what I had said, and asked
him if I meant it. The assistant assured him
that I did, and that it was very true. But again
and again the old man said it over, 'She says
her God cannot be sick, grow old, or die.' It
seemed as if it were a truth he wanted to grasp,
and longed to rest upon ; but it was too wonder-
ful for him. The assistant tried to impress that
and other truths upon him ; and he listened with
great interest, seeming to feel that if there

could be such a God, it would be well to worship him.

"When we came away, after I had mounted my pony, he took my hand in both of his, stroked and patted it as if I had been his little child, asked me to come again, and said that when he came to town he should certainly come to see us." A year later my mother visited the village again, and found the old man still living, though he had failed in mind and body. "He came tottering to see us," she writes, "and *shikoed*, that is, bowed as they do in worship, but without his heathen prayer. He said he had been very lonely for us : he had thought of us with loving regret, but he could not get to town to see us. I asked him if he had prayed to the God who is free from sickness, old age, and death. He said, 'Yes.' I asked him if he trusted in Jesus, and he said 'Yes ;' still I could not feel sure that he understood sufficiently who Jesus is to exercise a saving faith in him. Nevertheless I am not without hope that he may be saved."

At about the same time, my aunt met in the same village an old woman in whom she was greatly interested. She tried to talk with her, telling her she had come to bring her good

news, to show her the way in which she might
escape the evils of transmigration, they so much
dread, and attain a state far more desirable than
nigban. After putting forth Jesus as lovingly
as she could, she asked her if that was not good
news. You may judge how her heart fell to
hear her, though striving to be polite, indiffer-
ently reply, " If the teacher says it is good, it is
good." — " But do you not know it is good?"
— "Oh!" said she, " I am a woman : how can I
know any thing?" Thus we have encourage-
ments and discouragements ; our hearts now
tremble with hope, and now quiver with despair.
But still the word of the Lord is, " Go teach ; "
and what are we, that we should say it is in
vain? who knoweth which shall prosper, or
whether both shall be alike good? Again,
mother writes : " At another village, a crowd of
little girls gathered around me, and I wanted
very much to fix in their minds at least one
truth that day ; but I could not get them to
say a word. So I took out my Burman spell-
ing-book, showed them the letters, and tried to
have them call them after me, but still not a
word. Then I thought I would hire them, if
possible, for in some way I must reach them
with the truth. I hastily thought over every

thing I had with me, but could hit upon nothing transferable but a needle.   I held it up, and
asked who wanted that.   Several wistful eyes
were fastened upon it, but not a word was said.
I told them the one that would say the letters
after me should have it, and began calling them.
Soon in a whisper one of them said, '*kahghyee*,'
and then another whisper, till at last half a doz-
en voices were repeating the letters as nicely
as I could wish.   After going through the letters several times, I said I thought they had all
earned the needle, but, as it was only one, I
must give it to the one who spoke first : but
I found a pin-ball in my pocket, so I gave each of
the others a pin, the first, I suppose, they had
ever seen.   Observing the head, they wanted to
know what they must do with that : so I explained how they could fasten a jacket — sup-
posing they had one — with it, at which they
were greatly pleased.   I then took the catechism, and asked them the first question, ' Who
made the heavens and the earth and all things?'
Not one of them knew, as I expected.   So I
gave them the answer, making them repeat it,
and apply it to the various objects and animals
they could see, till I felt sure they would not
forget it.   Then I took the second question,

'Who is God?' and the answer, 'God is without beginning or end, eternally existing, forever established, unchangeably the same.' This I made them repeat again and again, till I thought they would remember the words, though they might not comprehend the meaning, even in a slight degree, till I came again. I did not burden their minds with any thing further that day. If they remember this one truth, that God made all things, I shall feel that the labor of the day was not in vain. You see how we have to work, beginning at the lowest possible point, giving line upon line, precept upon precept, till, were it not for the everlasting arms beneath, we should weary and despair."

If our ride was planned only for the morning, the increasing heat of the sun would soon force us to return; and, reaching home about nine o'clock, we ate our heartier breakfast.

From nine till four, my parents were occupied with varied work, preaching, teaching, receiving inquirers and other visitors, and explaining to them the religion of the living God. Of the number of things demanding the missionaries' attention, people here have but little idea. The missionary and his wife are not only teachers, but doctors and nurses for the sick, judges and lawyers for those who have any quarrel, and servants of all.

We dined at four o'clock, principally upon rice and curry; often upon soup, fowl, fish, and in some places we could obtain a piece of meat. A few vegetables, cucumbers, yams, tomatoes, and a poor quality of sweet-potatoes, were sometimes added.

The day closed as it began, in visiting the neighboring villages, distributing tracts, and sowing the seed of the kingdom.

Burman worship was always held in our house, at dark. This closed the public labors of the day. The natives do not venture out much at night; and it is not safe for any one to do so, unless provided with lantern or cane, on account of snakes and dogs. The weary missionary is only too glad to retire early, after a little reading and writing, in order to be ready for an early start the next morning.

The school was held for a time at the chapel, but was afterwards on our compound, and sometimes in both places. The scholars were gathered from the Burmans, Shans, and Eurasians, and were first taught to read and write the Burmese language. A Bible-lesson was given to the whole school daily, and there were classes in both Old and New Testaments. Even before they could read, every pupil was thoroughly taught the catechism prepared by the first Mrs. Judson, which was such an epitome of the saving truths of the gospel, that we felt sure, that having committed it to memory, even though they learned nothing else, they might, by the power of the Holy Spirit, be brought to Christ. They were further taught something of arithmetic, geography, and astronomy; the two last being especially useful in undermining the Buddhist religion. The average cost for each pupil was about five rupees, or two dollars and a half, per month. This includes board, clothing, books, and medicines. The most difficult part of their education is training them in habits of order and neatness. When they first enter school, all smoke cigars, and chew the betel-nut; and the giving up of these two practices costs them a great effort. They have very fixed and foolish ideas in regard to work; but they soon learn that no useful labor is degrading to Christian people. A prayer-meeting was held sabbath morning at six o'clock, preaching in Burmese at ten o'clock, Sunday school at one, and preaching again at five o'clock. In the evening another prayer-meeting fitly closed the day.

The school-work and preaching in town is
only one department of missionary labor, which
is carried on in the wet season, when the inces-
sant rains, swollen streams, and flooded roads
render travel impracticable. In the dry season
the missionaries travel among the mountains
and jungle-villages, preaching and distributing
tracts. My father had made several journeys
to the north of Toungoo, visiting people who
had never seen a white person until he went
among them. His journeys were often attended
with great danger; but he was repaid in being
able to plant churches, and supply them with
native preachers. These mountaineers and jun-
gle-people often came into town for purposes
of trade and to visit the missionaries. Negh-
yan, a mountain chief, with a large number of
followers, on such a visit, became acquainted
with Moung Ong, one of our most promising
Burman disciples, and greatly desired to take
him home with him as a teacher for his people.
My father asked Moung Ong if he were willing
to go. His countenance fell, and without reply-
ing he went away to his house. It would be a
great sacrifice for a comparatively refined, intelligent Burman to leave his home, and go to
dwell among those ruder savages. His life and

health would be imperilled; and, moreover, he would be cut off from the Christian influences and instruction which he was learning to prize. Moung Ong knew this, and a stern conflict was going on in his mind. The day wore away; and in the twilight he came to my father, and calmly said, "Teacher, when people are thirsty we must give them water, for when their thirst is gone they will not drink." Oh that all Christians would consider this! Is it possible that with the bread of life and the refreshing waters of salvation in our possession, we can withhold them from the millions now perishing? A few days later he started with the chief and his company, on his journey. One of the men bore upon his back the first whole copy of the Bible that had ever made its way up these mountains. It was a well of water at which many thirsty souls have been refreshed and saved. Moung Ong labored there a few years, was then taken ill, and came home. He died on our compound, and was buried in the mission burying-grounds. Not long after, my eldest brother was taken from us, and sorrowfully we laid him to rest by the side of Moung Ong. Their bodies lie side by side, the missionary child and the native Christian, while their spirits are "present with the Lord."

CHAPTER VIII.

Travel in Burmah.

Ten years ago there was not a single railroad in all Burmah, though now there is one from Rangoon to Prome. There were some cart-roads, but no good carriage-roads outside the large towns.

Journeys by land must be on elephants, in bullock or buffalo carts, or on ponies. The latter were chiefly used in all our mountain-travel; for through forests and over mountains we had only a narrow footpath, and were often obliged to cut away vines and branches to secure that. Once, when riding rapidly, a slender vine growing athwart our path caught one of our party across the shoulders; and a sudden, not to say surprising, sitting-down was the result. Sometimes, where the forests were dense, we were obliged to follow the bed of a stream for miles. On one trip we crossed the same river twenty times. Not far from home was a large stream, deep and with a strong current. It was necessary to cross by boat, holding the pony's head above water, and making him swim, careful to keep him on the upper side of the boat, so that the current might not carry the boat upon his back.

Father was once returning home, after an extended trip among the hills, and, on reaching the stream, found only a woman there to ferry him over. The pony had a special dislike for water, and obstinately refused to enter the stream. At length the idea seemed to come to him that home was on the other side. Suddenly he plunged in on the wrong side of the boat, swimming with such force as to carry every thing with him. Father held the reins, and the woman tried to steady the boat. As soon as the pony touched bottom, he rushed for the shore, dragging the boat, father still clinging to the reins. The woman was jerked off into the water; but hastily gathering up her falling robes, paddle in hand, she waded after. A representation of the scene were worthy the genius of a Nast.

When travelling in the jungle, we must be constantly on our guard against wild beasts and poisonous reptiles, especially if we are obliged to camp in the woods. The missionary then

pitches his tent ; or, if he is not so fortunate as
to have one, he constructs a bamboo shelter,
and builds a large fire in front. Then his
attendants form a circle around him, and build
other fires, which they keep burning all night.
If they sleep too soundly, and the fires die, they
are often roused by the crashing of a wild elephant among the trees, or by some mysterious
crackling of twigs and bushes ; and they speedily
renew the fires. If we stop for the night in a
village, the missionary and perhaps the native
preacher occupy the chapel, or the zayat built
for the accommodation of travellers. On one
occasion my father had fastened his ponies to
trees near by, and had retired for the night.
He was soon awakened by their stamping and
snorting : he hurried out to see what was the
matter. Immediately some wild beast bounded
away through the bushes. The men were soon
on the spot, shouting and pounding on the house
to frighten him still more. The footprints proved
it to be a tiger.

By water, we journeyed in the little boats
before described, subject to the caprices of indolent boatmen, and were often obliged to regulate
our course by the ebb and flow of the tide, lest
we be cast upon the quicksands or ingulfed in

A BURMAN ZAYAT.

a flood of water. The tide, as it comes up from the sea and bay into the Sitang River, finds its path suddenly narrowed, and in proportion as the space diminishes, the formerly gentle tide swells to a flood of angry waters many feet in height; and, as if enraged with its restrictions, the *dee*, or *bore*, rushes, with a headlong speed and a noise like thunder, up the river, carrying destruction for all that may come in its way. It is said that no ordinary ship could stand the force of this roaring, seething mass of water, which every twelve hours makes its way along these shores. It may be possible then to form some idea of our danger in our frail boat. The only way of escape is to turn aside, when time for the tide, into one of the many little creeks fortunately scattered along the river, and there wait till the *dee* has passed.

Never shall I forget the experience of one dreary night. The tide had been very low, and consequently our boat had run aground often, and we had been obliged to move slowly, so that darkness came upon us before we came to a creek. The time for the *dee* was approaching, and almost certain death was before us unless the creek could be reached. Often the boatmen were ready to despair, and to forsake all and escape to land; but my father urged them on with repeated assurances that a creek must be near. At last we heard the roar which signalled its approach. Though several miles distant, it would soon be upon us. What anxiety filled our hearts! What earnest prayers went up to the Ruler of the waves! And were not our prayers answered? We gained the creek, and had barely entered it when the *dee* thundered past. We soon entered the river again to take advantage of the current. Danger was still ahead. The night was dark. The boatmen who were propelling the boat by planting one end of the pole in the bank, and thus pushing the boat along, could not see where to put their poles; and at one time several tons of earth loosened and fell just as we passed from its reach. A little nearer, and it would have sunk the boat. Again, an old tree partly overhanging the bank fell within a few inches of our stern, and we were saved. My little brother's prayer that night had been, "*O Lord, take good care of us to-night, and don't let any thing bite us.*" We had occasion to remember that; for in the morning, when my father awoke, he discovered a large snake lying along the edge of the boat, where, if he had stretched out his arm, it would have bitten

him. We afterwards learned that early on this
fearful night a dear missionary whom we had
visited in Rangoon awoke feeling greatly trou-
bled about us. She awoke her husband, and
said, " Our friends are in trouble : we must pray
for them." And they did pray, scarcely sleeping
again until morning. It proved to be the time
when we were so wonderfully rescued from those
successive perils. " The angel of the Lord
encampeth round about them that fear him, and
delivereth them."

CHAPTER IX.

SHWAY-DA-GŌNG. — MAH MŌNG.

THERE are names the very mention of which opens the windows of imagination and the flood-gates of memory, and carries us swiftly through the scenes of joy or sorrow associated with them. The pulse of the whole world quickens at the word Rome. We think of her magnificence and power; we see the blood of the martyrs poured out; we tremble at the horrors of the inquisition; and we shrink from the thought of the spiritual thraldom in which she now holds thousands of devotees.

We speak of Mecca, and behold vast processions crossing burning deserts or threading lonely wilds, enduring suffering and even death, that they may kneel at that sacred shrine.

Washington, our own Washington!

"Breathes there the man with soul so dead
Who never to himself hath said,
'This is my own, my native land'?"

So the mention of Shway-da-Gōng sends a

PAGODA.

thrill to the heart of every Buddhist. Its power
is felt not only throughout Burmah, but in all
surrounding countries.   It is the Buddhist's
most sacred shrine. Eight hairs of Gaudama
are said to have been deposited beneath it when
it was built many hundred years ago ; and choi-
cest blessings are to be bestowed on those who
most frequently and devoutly bow before it.

Like our church-spires, the pagoda tapers, like
an uplifted finger, toward the skies ; but its
golden *H'tee* at the top turns downward again
to earth, — fit emblem of the reaching-up of
heathen hearts toward heavenly things, yet
crushed to earth again by the gilded shelter of
good works.

Nine pilgrimages to that pagoda entitle one
to annihilation, — the Buddhist's only heaven ;
and so the fond mother fastens her babe upon
her back, and toils on foot over mountains and
valleys, fording streams, pillowed by night on
the ground, and canopied by the sky, in the
hope that some time during his life her child
may make the requisite number of journeys,
counting this as one of them ; and, though she
may fail, he may attain the desired haven.   ·

See the pilgrims gather, — from all Burmah,
from Assam and Siam, from the numberless

mountain-tribes, from Shanland, and even from China; "these from the North, these from the South, and these from the land of Sinim" — to prostrate themselves before this mass of brick and mortar and outward gilding. When, O Immanuel! shall these multitudes turn unto thee as doves to their windows? Oh, hasten the time when the heathen shall be given thee as thine inheritance, and "the knowledge of the Lord shall cover the earth as the waters cover the sea"!

It is painful to witness the zeal of idolaters in worshipping their false gods. "Only yesterday," writes a missionary, "the streets were filled with an eager, excited throng, all wending their way to the pagoda. A new idol had just been brought from Mandelay, for which hundreds of rupees had been paid; and the crowd was going to see it placed in a niche of the pagoda." Never a day passes that the idol shrines are not filled with offerings of fruit and flowers and food. Beggars and lepers line the approaches. Heathen nuns, with shaven heads and white robes, hover around to clean the altars and sweep the walks, in order to gain merit. Aged men and women creep up the steps, and pluck every blade of grass growing between the bricks. Numbers of deluded worshippers are constantly prostrate before the various altars, and the murmur of their prayers is interrupted only by the frequent tones of the great bells.

Not long ago the king of Burmah, the father of the present king, Theebaw, placed a new *H'tee* upon this pagoda ; and, being a very meritorious deed, it drew together a great concourse of people. It had been said that whoever should put a *H'tee* upon Shway-da-gōng should become ruler of Pegu ; and, doubtless, some hope of political power, as well as religious merit, entered into the mind of the king.

The cost of this *H'tee* was estimated at about six lacs of rupees, or three hundred thousand · dollars. It consisted of a frame-work of iron covered with gold-plate. This frame was made of seven rings, or terraces, growing smaller towards the top : the diameter of the largest is twelve feet. Each of these rings is studded with gems ; but they are too small to be seen when on the top of the pagoda, three hundred and seventy-three feet from the ground.

The gem of greatest value is an emerald in the very top of the structure. The *H'tee* was carried in pieces from its landing-place to the pagoda ; and the road for a distance of two miles was covered with white cloth by a devout resident of the town. It was placed under a building erected for the purpose, enclosed by a railing, inside which only a favored few were permitted to enter. Four large golden candlesticks of elaborate workmanship, presents from the four queens at Mandelay, were placed on a stand near the *H'tee*, with many other costly gifts.

It remained on exhibition a month. During that time, two missionary ladies, assisted by two or three native Christians, distributed twenty thousand tracts among the strangers that came from all parts of the country. They spread mats in the little zayats built on either side the steps leading to the pagoda, and, seated upon low stools, talked to the crowd who gathered around. In only two or three instances was a tract destroyed. Numbers were probably carried to places where no preacher or white book has ever been. This was sowing seed by the wayside, and some of it will bring forth good fruit.

During these weeks of religious festivity, offerings of gold and silver were day by day poured into the treasury at the pagoda. The more lavishly money was spent on this occasion,

the greater merit would be attained. An old
woman would totter up to the railing, and, carefully unrolling her old soiled handkerchief, de-
posit a precious stone, or a roll of gold, the
savings of years. Mothers stripped the chains
and bracelets from their little ones, and divested
themselves of their own ornaments, while those
who had nothing else to give cut off their hair
for an offering ; and one poor old woman, in the
warmth of her zeal, cut off a finger, and burned
it up.

The pagoda from base to summit was incased
in a network of bamboos which made the
ascent comparatively easy. Many Europeans
scaled the height, and were rewarded by a magnificent view of the surrounding country. The
old *H'tee* was removed with great care, and received its full share of adoration. The storms
of centuries had not left it unscathed. It was
a poor, dilapidated piece of iron frame, with
scarcely a bit of gold remaining. Ring after
ring, the new *H'tee* was elevated, by a contriv-
ance of ropes and pulleys, to its place.

The day on which the first ring was to be
placed in its position, seventy thousand people
were estimated to be present. " Such a company and such a scene," writes a missionary,

"beggars description. When the signal was given to pull the ropes, men, women, and children seized them frantically, and slowly the car was raised above the heads of the excited multitude. Shouts and cheers of the wildest sort rent the air, which, mingled with the din of their horrible instruments of music, was almost deafening. Parents held their little ones high up in their arms, that they might not lose the sight. Men and women danced wildly about, waving their hands in response to the shouts and gesticulations of those who had ascended the frame-work of the pagoda. Old men and women, who had probably dragged their feeble limbs up the steep ascent for the last time, were prostrate on the ground, with hands clasped and eyes raised with such an intensity of desire and eagerness in their expression, as was painful in the extreme to witness. As the car rose higher and higher, the enthusiasm increased. It was near the top when a rope broke, then another. Is the judgment of God about to decend upon the heads of this guilty throng? It was a moment of terrible suspense. But no! vengeance is delayed; the remaining ropes hold fast. With a faint, suffocated feeling, we forced our way out of the crowd and down the steps. We felt as if the whole structure was about to fall in token of God's displeasure with idolatrous worship."

The next day, in attempting to replace the ropes that were broken, two Shans fell from the top, and were instantly killed. One old woman was crushed to death. Another made a vow that she would walk around the pagoda seven times; but before the seventh round was accomplished she fell and expired. Many such incidents occurred. Two children were born there, and their mothers were considered most fortunate beings.

At last the *H'tee* is fixed, the offerings ended, and the crowd dispersed; and Shway-da-gōng still stands, as before, a mass of brick and mortar and outward gilding. Like human merit, the foundation of the religion it symbolizes, it is the wonder and admiration and end of desire to multitudes; but it saves none, and has no power to bless mankind.

Pagodas are scattered throughout Burmah and in all Buddhist countries. They are the monuments of Gaudama, the visible indications of his present power over the hearts of men. Paganism and the various forms of false religion have need to mark their existence by material

symbols : they make no change in men. The
heart that is impure and unholy when it embraces
Buddhism, Brahminism, or Mohammedanism, is
impure and unholy still. It produces no change
in life, and in death it gives no light.

What are thy monuments, O Christ? What
marks thy presence and power among men?
Come with me to our unobtrusive, ungilded,
unornamented chapel in Toungoo. It is sabbath
morning. Behold, among the natives gathered
there, a woman pale and weary ; beside her are
two little girls, also tired, travel-stained, and
footsore. They are Shans. A neighbor of
theirs last year came down to Toungoo, and
was employed by my father to take care of his
pony. In doing this, he heard the truth, and
was converted ; and like Andrew and Philip,
who quickly made known the Messiah they had
found, he wrote back to his native village that
there was a teachèr in Toungoo who knew the
way to heaven ; and that he had found that way,
and it was very good. He urged them all to
come, and enter with him that blessed way.
This woman, a widow, with her two little daugh-
ters and several neighbors, at once came down.
They were obliged to steal away ; for the Burman
king, to whom the Shan States are tributary, had

all the roads guarded by soldiers to prevent the
emigration of Shan families to the mild, attractive government of British Burmah. They hid
in the jungle by day, and made their way cau-
tiously through it by night, till they were out of
the territory of the Burman king. They were
the first of their race to undertake a religious
journey, not to worship at pagodas, but to hear
of Jesus. The mother soon sickened and died;
but the daughter, some years after, when she
was a Christian, said of her, "I think my mother
is in heaven, for she believed in Jesus as soon
as she heard of him."

My mother took the little girls, — Mah Mōng
and Mah Shway, — and taught them the way of
life their mother had brought them so far to
learn. They were both converted. Mah Shway
married a Shan disciple, and is still living, a
faithful, loving wife, a devoted mother, and useful Christian. Mah Mōng married a Burman
disciple, and, with him, engaged in service in
the family of an English officer. So faithful
and trustworthy were they, that, when the family
left Burmah for India, they took them with them.
After a few years they returned to Burmah,
bringing with them their only child, a little boy,
the delight of both their hearts. This little boy

was not taught to fold his hands, and worship idols, but to lisp the name of Jesus, and to repeat the sweet words, "Suffer little children to come unto me." When four years of age, just when he was most closely twined with every fibre of his mother's heart, one of the many diseases that prey upon little ones there fell upon him. Mah Mōng did not shriek, tear her hair, or rend her garments; but, sustained by the love of Christ, stronger than any earthly love, she sat by his side, and told him the way of life. When he felt the chill touch of death, his little heart shrank, and he said, "I 'fraid, mamma." Choking back her tears, she said, "Do not be afraid, my darling. The Saviour calls you: he wants you in his beautiful home above." And the little child, assured and comforted, went to be with Jesus.

Mah Mōng was ever ready to do what she could to make known the glad tidings to her people. She was the companion and friend of missionaries. Said one who was with her in her last days, "We all loved Mah Mōng so much. She was like a sister to me." But her health failed, and she was called to endure a long and painful illness. She was a most patient sufferer, grieving most of all that the time necessarily spent in caring for her could not be devoted to teaching those who were not Christians ; and, when the missionary mamma put off her jungle-trip to remain with her, she said, " O mamma, I am so long in dying! If I could go home now, you could go to the jungle, and carry the good news."

As the missionary was entering her room one day, she heard her praying, and paused at the door. She was saying, " O Lord, let thy will be done. Thou knowest how long I have suffered, and how glad I shall be to come to Thee. Call me now, if Thou canst. Thy will, not mine, be done." The missionary was not well ; and Mah Mōng quickly noticed her pale face, and tenderly urged her to take medicine, that she might be strong to tell her people the way of life. When the missionary went in the next day, her husband said, " Mah Mōng had a peculiar experience last night. She awoke me by making a strange noise. I asked her what was the matter. She said, ' I am trying to sing. My heart is full of light. Oh, I am so happy! I thought I had arrived at the heavenly city. The door was open, and I saw the golden streets, and an angel came out and talked with me. He said, " You must wait a little, Mah Mōng.

The Lord will call for you after Christmas." I asked him about the mamma: would she come soon? but I could not hear what he said about her.'" And so said she to the mamma, "Do not put off the Christmas-tree," referring to Christmas plans that were likely to be deferred on account of her precarious state: "I shall not die till after Christmas, and I want you all to have a good time." So the Christmas gathering was held, and those who made presents remembered her. The morning after, the missionary carried Mah Mōng's presents to her. Her face was full of joy. She received the presents gratefully, and said, "How kind every one is to me! These are beautiful presents; but one thought of the home to which I am going is worth more than all these, and I am going soon now." The next day she heard the call, and went up higher. Such are thy monuments, O Prince of Peace! When Shway-da-gōng shall have crumbled into smallest dust, Mah Mōng "shall shine as the brightness of the firmament and as the stars for ever and ever."

CHAPTER X.

THE FIRST SEPARATION. — BOGHYEE. — MOUNG SEE DEE. —
THE PADOUNGS.

My first experience of the great trial — separation from parents — which sooner or later
must darken the life of every missionary child,
was in the dry season of 1864, when my father
and mother made the first missionary journey
to the Shan States. They committed my baby
brother and myself to the care of kind missionary friends, at whose house we all passed the
night previous to their departure.

Well do I remember the events of the following morning. After a hasty breakfast we gathered in front of the house. There were the
ponies upon which my father and mother were
to ride, the Burman and Karen preachers who
were to assist in proclaiming the truth, and the
coolies with their baskets of provisions and
books.

Conspicuous among them all was the venerable San Quala, who always reminded me of

David of the Old Testament, or Paul of the
New, ready to give his parting benediction, re-
joicing that still farther into his darkened coun
try the light of life was to penetrate.   A hymn
was sung; Rev. Mr. Cross then fervently com-
mended the travellers to loving Omnipotent
care; a last kiss was bestowed upon baby fast
asleep in his *pakett*, and upon the tearful little
girl standing near, and they were gone.   Should
we ever see them again?   Yes, sooner than we
expected; for, having penetrated to the borders
of Shan-land, a mutiny of the coolies compelled them most unwillingly to abandon the
journey, and return to Toungoo.

On their way back, they were met by Boghyee, the most powerful of Geckho chiefs, who
said, " Why do you go to the Shans?   They are
a bad people; they have no truth: why do you
not preach to us?   My people have not heard
your law so much as once.   Preach to me."
My father began by telling of God, the creation,
the first human beings, pure and holy, their fall,
and the consequent sin, sorrow, suffering, and
death of the human race.   To all this Boghyee
assented.   *" Koung-deh, koung-deh,"* said he,
"it is good, your words are very true: we have
all sinned, we all have sorrow and suffering, and

A PAKETT OR BURMAN CRADLE.

must die." My father went on to say, that, while in this present state all men were in very much the same condition, in the future state there would be a difference : there was a world of woe, and a heaven of eternal glory. The old man eagerly interrupted, "*Koung-ghin lan pyah bah, pyah bah, ter youk ghyn the.*" "Show me, show me the road to heaven : I very much want to arrive there."

My father then preached to him Christ, the way to eternal life. He received the truth with gladness. "You must come to my village," said he. "I have twenty villages. We will build a chapel in every village, and my people will learn books and worship God."

My father heard these words with feelings of mingled gladness and grief ; glad that a spirit of inquiry was given to these hearts, and grieved that he had not a man to send, or the means to support him there.

But behold the hand of God! Among the letters in Toungoo, awaiting his arrival, was one from a gentleman residing in Rochester, N.Y. He had earnestly desired in early life to be a missionary, but circumstances had prevented. His heart was in the work, and he wished to have some one preach for him among the hea-

then.   He would not ask for a Paul or an Apol-
los; but for "a good man, full of faith and the
Holy Ghost," the funds for whose support he
would gladly furnish.   Here were the means.

He also found awaiting him a young man, a
Karen by birth, who had spent two years at the
theological school in Rangoon.   He spoke Burmese fluently, as well as several Karen dialects,
and was anxious to work for the Master wher-
ever he was needed.   Here was the man; not
twenty men, but one man; and in these coinci-
dences the leading hand of God was manifest.

This young man, Moung See Dee, was sent
as soon as possible to Shway-nan-ghyee, one of
the principal Geckho villages, where he entered
upon his life-work of preaching and teaching
the gospel, and the people gathered about him
with confidence and regard.   To encourage the
women and girls to learn, my mother told him
she would give a Testament and jacket to every
one of them who learned to read the Bible.
Before the end of the dry season, Moung See
Dee came down to Toungoo, attended by a
group of Geckhos; and among them six girls
came to claim the promised gift.   It was a day
never to be forgotten.   I thank God it was
given to me, as a little child, to hear their low

voices timidly reading the second chapter of Matthew, to prove their right to the prize, and to see put into their hands the first copies of his Word ever any woman of their tribe had owned.

The jackets were of calico, a yard and a half in each. They were of very little real value; but in their eyes, when the promise was first made to them, worth more than many Bibles.

The word of God has never yet returned void. Ere long my father was called upon to organize, at this village, the first church among the Geckhos. A beautiful group was baptized, among them the chief's daughter, one of the six above mentioned, who afterwards became the young preacher's wife.

Several other chapels were opened among these tribes, when my father was obliged to leave the country. The Rev. Mr. Bunker then took charge of this field, to whom we are indebted for further accounts of Moung See Dee's — now called Th'rah Tah Dee[1] — interesting work.

[1] The various races of Burmah have no family names, and the names by which they are called are changed according to ²-age, situation, and circumstances. Moung See Dee is the Burman name by which he was known as a young man. Moung is a general appellation, meaning brother. Th'rah means teacher, and he is now known as Teacher Tah Dee.

After this church at Shway-nan-ghyee was well established, Tah Dee was anxious to push into new regions, and took up his abode in a very wild village called Prai-so, a full day's journey beyond. After two or three years' work here, a church was organized; and, after settling a pastor over it, Th'rah Tah Dee again pushed on This time he crossed the watershed range of mountains, between the Salwen and Toungoo Rivers, which had never before been crossed by a religious teacher, save once by my father and his company, years before. This range runs north and south. Passing over it towards the east, you look down into a long, narrow valley of peculiar beauty.

The boundaries of several tribes meet here ; and Tah Dee, perceiving how important a position this valley would be in the advance of Christianity, established himself at a Padoung village called Wah-thaw-ko.

These Padoungs are a very interesting people, and, until Tah Dee went among them, very few had heard the name of Jesus.

The first to hear the glad tidings came down to Toungoo with the Geckho chief Neeghyan, on one of his visits to my father. He started to return with him ; but after two days' journey he left the company, and came back to Toungoo. He gave the reason for this step as follows : "He had pondered by the way, the things he had heard of the teacher : they had deeply impressed his mind ; he wanted to know more about them. He was the first of his tribe who had heard about Jesus Christ, and he wanted all his people to hear. He did not understand enough to be their teacher ; but he thought if he came back to the teacher, and studied books, he would soon be able to teach his people, and perhaps he could persuade the teacher to go home with him when the rains were over." Father gladly took him into school. He was a sprightly young man about twenty-five years of age, and spoke Shan perfectly. He gave interesting descriptions of his people. After studying a while, he reluctantly went back to his country as a guide to a party of travellers ; but he soon returned, bringing with him six of his countrymen.

Some time after this, while at a mountain village, a Padoung chief and seven men visited my father. They had never seen a white person ; and, when they had a fair view of him, the old chief exclaimed, "*Amai! amai!* is it possible such men can be good ?" Three of the number were persuaded to shake hands; but the others turned their backs, and no amount of persuasion could win them.

There are about nineteen thousand Padoungs, distributed in sixty-two villages. The tribe is very thrifty, and their villages are permanent. Their country is from seven thousand to eight thousand feet above the sea, and has a comparatively cool climate, and the people are more robust than their neighbors. When the missionary first visited this people, their villages were surrounded by stockades and ditches, and the whole country was in a state of feudal war. Tah Dee labored for several years, and in 1876 the Rev. Mr. Bunker organized the first church among the Padoungs. He found then no stockade or ditch around the village. He saw no frightened people, with arms for protection, save as he visited other villages in the neighborhood. There were eleven young men and women awaiting baptism. Peace had come into the beautiful valley, and war had retired to the hills about. A good schoolhouse and chapel had been erected; and altogether the changes that had been wrought by Tah Dee, as an instrument in the hands of the Holy Spirit, were truly inspiring. Last accounts give more

baptisms and evidences to show that the light
is reaching many villages.

Tah Dee has made many and extended journeys throughout the Padoung country, and we
may confidently expect a large harvest from
this people in the future. He has peculiar
qualifications for pioneer-work. He is a born
leader and a good organizer. He is a brave
man, and entirely weaned from the superstitions
of his people. He has been instrumental, altogether, in the planting of ten churches, and
there is great hope of future usefulness. Has
not the gentleman in Rochester, who was the
means of putting Th'rah Tah Dee into the field,
found that which he asked for, "a good man,
full of faith and the Holy Ghost"? Has he not
through him abundantly preached the gospel
to the heathen? After some years this gentleman's health failed; and he reluctantly consented that the Cranston-street Sunday school,
in Providence, R.I., should furnish Tah Dee's
support, which they still gladly do. Mr. Phin-
ney was not a rich man; but he brought a few
loaves to Christ, and thousands have been fed.
Will not other men and other Sunday schools
do likewise?

CHAPTER XI.

SEVEN WEEKS UPON THE MOUNTAINS.

No period of my child-life in Burmah do I recall with greater interest than the seven weeks
I spent among the mountains lying to the north-
east of my home. Upon their wooded depths
and dusky outline I had often gazed with a kind
of awe, wondering what of life was hidden there;
and great was my delight as I heard talked over
the plans of a jungle-trip in which I was includ-
ed. These mountains are the homes of various Karen tribes, — Bghais, Geckhos, Saukoos,
Brecs, Harshwees, Padoungs, and Red Karens;
and beyond these lie the Shan States, called in
our school-geographies " Laos."

We left home early in the morning, my father, my aunt, and myself, accompanied by two
native preathers and several coolies. Our provisions, cooking-utensils, beds, and books were
carried by the coolies in bamboo baskets sus-
pended from bamboo poles borne across their
shoulders. These poles are the lifelong com-

panions of the coolies, and to them they profess very great attachment. An indignity offered to the coolie's bamboo is resented much more promptly and severely than if offered to his mother. He says he loves his bamboo just as much as he does his mother, his wife, or his child.

We travelled about twenty miles the first day. A large part of the way lay over a burning plain, with the sun almost over our heads. Then we entered shady forests, our narrow pathway winding along the banks of a river, where our eyes were constantly delighted by the heavy foliage and beautiful flowers. Occasionally we were obliged to stop to cut away vines and branches, or to climb over some large tree fallen across the path. At three o'clock we arrived at Karen Khyoung, the first in the line of Christian villages which now dot the way to the Shan States, and made ourselves comfortable in the little zayat. No sooner had we spread our mats, and seated ourselves, than we were surrounded by the villagers ; and the rest of the day was passed in preaching, singing, and teaching.

Early the next morning we proceeded on our journey, and soon began to climb our first mountain, called Pan Doung, or Flower Mountain. Its summit was a fair garden of the Lord, covered with a charming variety of wild flowers, ferns, and trees. At noon we rested by the side of a dashing mountain-stream, the water of which was delightfully cool.

The chief of Kyah Maing, the next village, met us here. He and his people had received the teacher coolly on his first visit, and demanded exorbitant prices for all supplies. Now he welcomed him with the affection of a son, and sent back at once for an elephant to take up our baskets.

We stopped for the night on an elevation at the foot of Long-Rock Mountain, so called because of a large granite rock upon it, thirty-four feet high. It is shaped like a sugar-loaf, and on its top were growing beautiful orchids whose heavy blossoms we would fain have gathered. At its foot were a multitude of ferns and flowers in all their wealth of tropical delicacy, luxuriance, fragrance, and color; but my aunt was more moved by a single monotropa (as we call it in America, the Indian pipe, but which the natives of Burmah call English pipe) growing in an old paddy-field. Such is the charm of early association and native land.

While quietly resting we heard a distant shout far above us. My father recognized the call, and replied. It was soon followed by another; and, guided by responding shouts, a company of ten men made their way to our camp. They were disciples from Kyah Maing. They heard of our coming on their return from their paddy-fields at dark; and, after eating rice, they came through the dense jungle, a distance of at least six miles, to help us on our way in the morning. It was pleasant to receive such cordial greetings in those dark wilds.

After some hard climbing the next morning, we reached the village, about three thousand feet above the Toungoo plain. There we found ourselves literally above the clouds. A dense fog filled the plain beneath. So it is in this world's plain : dark, cold, and cheerless are the clouds that often hang over the soul. It is impossible for us to see the bright sunlight above, where God perpetually shines; but we may rest assured that the Sun of righteousness and truth will soon dispel the clouds, and the clear, beautiful blue of God's unchanging love, our eternal canopy, will be revealed.

The people were joyful at our coming; and the whole village, bearing rice, fruit, and flowers, came out in procession to welcome us. Each one gave us a cordial shake of the hand. I had seen representatives of these tribes in town, but to meet them on their native hills was a new experience. Their whole appearance was novel and striking. They were stouter and stronger than the people in the plains; they were ruder in manners and dress, more timid, and yet more confiding and thoughtful of strangers. The men wore only a simple tunic, reaching to the knee. The women wore a short skirt of many colors, and an upper tunic of mingled cotton and bright red silk, all of their own manufacture.

We took up our abode in the chapel, and remained here four days. During the day, men, women, and children worked hard in the rice-fields; but morning and evening they gathered for instruction. Late on Saturday evening we heard the people pounding rice. They had been in the field all day, and were now working till near midnight to prepare their food, so that they might rest on the Lord's Day.

At the early morning prayer-meeting between fifty and sixty were present. We met in the middle of the day for preaching and Bible-study, and again in the evening for preaching. Several gave evidence of conversion.

TRAVELLING BY ELEPHANT.

A BAPTISM. 139

On Monday the head-man of Lapet Ing
came over with his elephant to take us to his
village, where we met a warm reception. We
occupied a temporary house built for us by the
people. Here we found a large company of
Shan traders, direct from the Shan country,
going with their wares, ponies, and cattle to
Rangoon and other towns in British Burmah.
These Shans have been called "the merchant-
princes of Burmah;" but certainly not on account of any princely bearing. Their appearance was uncouth and wild, but my father
spoke to them of the love of Christ.

On Thursday we returned to Kyah Maing,
to meet again the band of young converts;
and, after a careful examination, thirteen were
accepted as candidates for baptism. Difficulty
was found in preparing a baptistery. Men
worked hard to make a dam across a mountain-stream, but were disappointed on Sunday
morning to find the water would not stay. It
was decided that we must go a long distance to
the foot of the mountain. After singing and
prayer at the chapel, we started down the hill.
Looking back from the foot of a steep descent,
we saw the whole village filing down the narrow path, the men with their blankets thrown

loosely about their shoulders, and the women in their bright-colored tunics, — all solemn, yet cheerful and happy. The baptistery was in the bed of a large, cold mountain-stream, which ran through a deep, wild gorge, from which the banks rise almost perpendicularly to a dizzy height, covered with heavy timber and bamboo thickets, through whose closely locked branches it seems as if the sunshine could never penetrate. A solemn stillness rested here, broken only by the murmur of the stream. Very sweetly sounded the voice of praise and prayer, as they rang out for the first time in this wild mountain pass. Our hearts melted as our dusky brethren and sisters were buried with Christ in baptism, and came forth to a new life in him.

> " Blest be the tie that binds
> Our hearts in Christian love."

In the evening the Lord's Supper was administered to about eighty. The collection amounted to fourteen rupees, or seven dollars. It was a delightful day to all.

The next morning we bade farewell to this warm-hearted people. The chief took our baskets on his elephant ; and we went to Ko Aik's village, and spent the night. The women of

these villages are usually shy ; but the presence
of the white lady and child gave them assur-
ance, and we always had a lively group about us.

The last day of the closing year found us at
Shway-nan-ghyee. It was pleasant to contrast
our reception with that my father met on his
first visit. Most remarkable changes had taken
place. Then he was compelled to cut his way
to the villages through tangled thickets, often
thickly planted with poisoned spikes, and was
received with spears, bows and arrows, guns,
and sullen faces. Now, how different! We
find good roads and warm Christian friends,
who hailed our coming as a joyful event, and
supplied all our wants without price.

Here we had the pleasure of witnessing the
removal of an entire village. Those who have
experienced the protracted bustle and labor of
a New-England moving of a single family will
scarcely believe me when I say that a whole
village in one day changed their place of residence, and by night were resting as quietly as
if nothing had transpired. The people of this
village suffered greatly from malaria, owing to
their unhealthy location. My father helped
them to select a suitable place ; and the next
day they collected their families, and prepared

for their journey. Their baggage was light.
All the clothes they possessed were those they
had on ; and their articles of furniture would all
be made new, clean, and fresh, from portions of
the bamboos now growing where in a few days
their houses would stand. A few of the men,
armed with large knives, spears, bows and
arrows, led the way with the droves of buffaloes.
In single file they descended the steep moun-
tain-side ; and we followed on our ponies, with
our party. After us came the women and children, while another band of armed men closed
up the rear.

For several hours we descended, sometimes
amused and entertained by their wild mountain
songs, and now and then stopping to rest in
some lovely nook. At the foot of the mountain
was a deep, wide ditch half full of mud ; and it
required no little care to see the whole procession safely across. The easiest way for us was
to make our ponies leap over. My father and
myself landed safely on the other side ; but my
aunt's pony became frightened, and, missing his
foothold, sank floundering in the mire.

One of the natives immediately sprang in, and
seized the bridle to guide the animal ; but, wheel-
ing suddenly, he gave the man an unexpected

push, so that he was compelled to take a very humble seat, which, though soft, was not agreeable. We shall never forget the look of injured innocence with which he gazed up at us before he could recover himself sufficiently to rise.

Having crossed this Slough of Despond, we commenced the ascent of the mountain, which was long and tedious, often leading over heights which seemed almost perpendicular.

Late in the afternoon we gained the site of the new village, a beautiful place. We looked down upon fleecy clouds floating like a veil between us and the valley where our feet so lately trod. Around us, as far as eye could see, rose range after range of mountains, over which soft lights and shadows played.

> " Methinks it should have been impossible
> Not to love all things in a world so filled,
> Where the breeze warbles, and the mute, still air
> Is music slumbering on her instrument."

But the natives could not linger to admire the lovely landscape. They turned their faces to the waving forest of bamboos, where they must prepare themselves shelter for the night. They began to fell trees, and soon had a space cleared, where they constructed little bamboo booths for immediate use. In the evening, gathered in groups, they seated themselves upon the ground around the different fires. The women had been busy gathering the long dry grass, and were now tying it to strips of split bamboo stems about three or four feet in length, that they might be in readiness to roof the houses, which must be begun on the morrow. The men took tall, slender bamboos, and splitting them into thin, smooth strips about three inches in width, wove them in and out to form a matting, which they would use for the walls.

We slept that night on the ground, lulled to rest by the wind in the trees and by the buzz and hum of the myriad insects ; and all night long the twinkling stars looked at us through our leafy bower, and kept their silent watch.

Early in the morning the men went to work in the forest, while the women prepared the breakfast. For utensils they turned to their never-failing friend, the bamboo. Selecting one about six inches in diameter, they divided it just below each joint, thus obtaining a vessel two or three feet in length, open at the top, perfectly tight, and possessing in itself a sweet, delicate flavor, which is no detriment to the food. Filling this one-third full of rice, with a little water, they placed it in the fire, resting it in an inclined position on a horizontal pole. The bamboo, being green, does not burn. When the rice is cooked, they cut the bamboo open lengthwise, and, laying open the two parts, had their rice all ready. It was a breakfast which cannot be equalled in this country.

Among those tribes which had begun to receive Christian ideas, it was pleasant to notice their respect for God evinced in many ways. In building their village, for instance, they erected God's house before they commenced their own.

The chapel was to be the centre of the village. They first placed in the ground four tall bamboo posts. About fifteen feet from the ground, they fastened to these posts, on each side, other bamboos placed horizontally. Across these they laid smaller pieces of bamboos, fastened closely together by natural strings of reeds growing abundantly with the bamboos and grass. This is the floor. The walls were made by tying to the upright posts the bamboo matting already mentioned. For the roof they fastened the dry thatch, prepared by the women, to the bamboo rafters, and the chapel was done.

The native houses were made in the same general way.

There is hardly a tree in the world so useful and necessary to man as the bamboo to these mountaineers. It often grows in symmetrical clusters, varying in diameter at their base from six to thirty feet or more. For about eight or ten feet from the ground, each of these clusters presents a form nearly cylindrical; after which they begin gradually to swell outwards, each bamboo assuming for itself a graceful curve, and rising often to the height of eighty or one hundred feet, the extreme end drooping lightly. It bears fruit at long intervals, and the leaves are narrow and small. Articles of furniture are made from it, also umbrellas, hats, musical instruments, baskets, cups, brooms, pipes, pens, bows and arrows, and wicks of candles. Its fine fibre is made into twine; its leaves are employed as a cloak in wet weather. The pulp is formed into paper, tender shoots are boiled and eaten, or made into pickles and sweetmeats, and its thick juice is said to be an excellent medicine. Indeed, it would be more difficult to say what the bamboo is not used for, than what it is. Through life the native is dependent upon it for support, he is borne upon it to his last resting-place, and its waving branches mark his tomb.

A KAREN CHAPEL.

It did not take our villagers long to become established in their new homes, and they were soon ready to work in their rice-fields.

We were surprised one night by a visit from Moung Doo, a savage old chief, who lived a distance of two days' journey from Shway-nanghyee, and who had long been the terror of the country. He had previously made friendship with my father. He reached this village at dark, and said that he dreamed the white teacher had arrived, and came to see if it were true. He manifested the greatest delight on seeing the teacher, taking hold of him with both hands, and shaking him heartily, exclaiming, "*Ro-ro-ro*" ("Good, good, good"). He repeated this salutation several times during the evening.

On the sabbath our worship was held in open air, the congregation sitting upon the ground in a half-circle. Never was there a more attentive audience. At the second service my father spoke to them for two hours, then they bowed reverently in prayer; and when the hymn "Come to Jesus, just now," was sung, young and old joined in the chorus, the children covering their faces with their hands, that they might not be seen. Their pastor, Th'rah Tah

Dee, had been very successful in teaching them to sing.

After visiting other villages, we returned to Lapet Ing, where my father left my aunt and myself for a few days. We staid in the house of one of the native Christians — if I may dignify by the name of house what seemed a large box, elevated upon bamboo posts, ten or twelve feet from the ground. The interior contained a single large room, with no opening, save the entrance, for the admission of light or air, and no chimney. It was occupied by five families, — fourteen persons besides children. Each family had a fireplace of its own ; and, as the nights were chilly, the fires were often kept burning until near morning, the smoke meanwhile creeping along the rafters, penetrating every corner, settling to the floor, and bringing abundant, though griefless, tears to our eyes. The only ornaments were lovely cobwebs spun in the corners, and festoons of soot which hung from ceiling and wall with a natural grace. The most cheery corner was given to us, and with our curtains and mats we made ourselves quite comfortable.

One night we were awakened by a great chattering and laughing, and, on inquiring the cause,

MOUNTAIN HOUSE.

discovered that there had been an addition to the family, and we were lulled to sleep again by the cries of the new arrival. We were surrounded every day by women and children, and we hope some seeds of truth were planted in their minds.

We had taught a young Shan Christian, who accompanied us, to prepare our simple meals. One day we thought we should enjoy a change, and, instead of our usual rice and curry for breakfast, would have grilled chicken. We called Toonlah, and explained to him that we were weary of *"hen"* (curry), and would like a chicken grilled. He assented, and hastened out to meet our wishes. After waiting an hour we felt hungry, and went out to find him. There he sat on the ground before the fire, with the plucked chicken in his hands, his face wearing a most doleful expression. He looked up, as we approached, heaved a deep sigh, and said, "Grill ter ket-the-go, hen ter lwai deh," "To grill is very hard, but to make curry is very easy." We allowed him to make the curry.

After my father rejoined us, we visited several other villages, among them that of Neeghyan, a powerful Geckho chief. On one of my father's visits there, he found Neeghyan and his brother.

very ill with cholera. The brother was then past hope of recovery; but my father undertook to save the chief. "O teacher!" said he, "if you will only save me, I will build a chapel, and have a teacher; and we will all learn your law, and worship the living God." Our God blessed the remedies, answered prayer, and the chief recovered. He kept his promise, built a chapel, and came down to Toungoo after Moung Ong, as before described. After some months of study, he came to town again, and with earnestness said, "Teacher, this religion is good. I want you to come up, and baptize my whole village." Interesting groups were from time to time converted and baptized, but the chief had recently died. His wife and brother were ruling in his place, and received us kindly.

We learned some of the circumstances respecting Neeghyan's burial, which were interesting. For the coffin, a tree was felled, a slab was cut off from one side, and it was then hollowed out to receive the body. They had buried with him eight pants, eight jackets, and eight turbans, saying, "So may he have plenty of clothing in the world to which he has gone." Six *dahs* (knives), one silver-plated, three spears, and five guns were added: so may he have

plenty of weapons. One *keezee*, one gong, fifteen rupees, two strings of precious stones, and
three pairs of silver bangles : so may he abound
in these things in the world to which he has
gone.

They killed four buffaloes, and placed the
heads in the grave; also the heads and feet of
fourteen pigs and six fowls, that he might not
lack for food in his new abode. At first we
were surprised at this; for we hoped he, and
others in the village, had accepted Christ as
their portion here and forever. But we soon
found, that, while believing in Jesus for the for-
giveness of sins and the saving of their souls, it
seemed too much to them that he should supply
all their wants. They had yet to learn that in
him "all fulness dwells."

They were not very unlike many professing
Christians here, who seem willing enough to
have Christ forgive their sins and save their
souls, but wish to spend all their time here in
adding to their possessions, beautifying their
homes, and making and arranging their dress.
These more simple natives thought only to pro-
vide for the future, as well as the present.

The people here are profusely ornamented.
The chief's wife took my aunt and me aside, and

displayed her jewels. She had ornaments for the ears, of gold, silver, and brass; chains of beads, precious stones, and silver coins, for the neck; bracelets for the arms; bangles and brass ornaments for the ankles and limbs. We spoke of some articles as very pretty, when, with a little toss of the head, she replied, "Oh, no! they are not pretty." She next called our attention to some nice blankets, by saying they were not very good; but would doubtless have been disappointed, had we expressed the same opinion. At last she brought forward a box containing a hymn-book, several tracts, and portions of the Scriptures. These were treasures indeed, which she was learning to prize.

The whole village came together in the evening, and listened attentively to the preaching. At the close, the chief's wife turned to the people, and told them "to consider what had been said, for the words were delightful."

We then visited Bo-ghy-ee, the Geckho chief mentioned in the preceding chapter. He was a fine-looking old man of about eighty years of age. His bearing was majestic and dignified. He said, "I am an old man, but I want to learn your law."

We thought that among the Geckho women

the love of finery had reached its utmost limit; for in addition to strings of beads, glass, and buttons around the neck, and ear-rings and finger-rings, they wore coils of brass wire as large as the little finger, reaching from the ankle to the knee, seven pounds weight sometimes on each foot. But here at Boghyee's, we found some Padoungs who had been driven from their villages, and had taken refuge here. Among them the mania for brass wire was much more evident. Besides the heaviest leg-ornaments, they commence in infancy to coil this brass or lead wire around the neck, increasing the number of coils from time to time. On an adult I counted thirteen coils on the neck and eight spreading on the shoulders. These are never removed; and the wearers are obliged to carry the head, with chin elevated, in such a position that they cannot see the ground on which they tread. The weight of brass on one person is often forty pounds. My aunt and I gazed at them, and they at us, with mutual astonishment. We were the first white women they had seen. They covered their faces with their hands, peeped at us between their fingers, keeping up a constant chatter, and uttering queer exclamations. At length they grew bold enough to draw near us, and touch our hands and faces to see if the white would not rub off. They won- dered if we were so white all over, and actually asked me to take off my shoes and stockings. I told them it was not our custom to remove them before people, and they did not urge it. Natives of the East are very polite, and never ask us to do what we say is not our custom.

While we were at this village, Boghyee offered to purchase me for one *keezee*, while his nephew offered three *keezees*. A *keezee* is a kind of gong made of bell-metal, and worth from fifty to six hundred rupees. They are manufactured by Shans, and are sometimes inlaid with gold: such are very handsome and expensive. These mountaineers invest their property in *keezees*.

These tribes are very different from the Bur- mans and Shans, who are Buddhists. Instead of worshipping idols of wood and stone, these tribes pay homage to spirits, both good and evil, which they believe to be constantly hovering around them. They believe in one supreme good spirit and one evil spirit, each attended by countless myriads of subordinates. Whenever illness or misfortune attends them, they consider it a punishment for some misdemeanor, and im- mediately offer some costly sacrifice to appease the spirit's wrath. One old man, whose wife was very ill, said to my father, " I have offered one buffalo, ten hogs, five dogs, and thirty fowls ; but the *nats* are still angry with me, and my wife does not recover. Now pray to your God, and see if he is able to save her." He did pray, and gave her medicine, and in a short time she was much better. When the old man saw her returning to health, he exclaimed, " Teacher, I'll never worship the *nats* again ! I will trust in God and medicine."

Although uncivilized and warlike as a people, they possess many noble qualities ; and those who enjoy the privileges afforded by the mission schools often astonish the teachers by their rapid progress, sometimes proving themselves capable of profound thought and reasoning. They are very fond of music ; and, although they have no musical system of their own, they learn very quickly to sing the Christian hymns taught by the missionaries.

We, who have enjoyed the blessings of Christianity all our lives, cannot realize the joyful changes which it brings to these benighted ones. The chief of Shway-nan-ghyee said to us, " Before the gospel was brought to us, we never slept in our village at this season of the year. We

were not afraid during the rains; but, when the
dry season came, we always hid about in the
jungles."

They lived in a state of constant fear, always
going well armed, and sleeping upon their arms
at night.

In a letter to "The Missionary Magazine," in
March, 1863, my father writes, "The divine
light is spreading; it has already reached some
of the Shan mountains, and the time is not far
distant when it will shoot across the country to
the land of Sinim.   'Behold, these shall come
from far, and lo, these from the north and from
the west, and these from the land of Sinim'
(Isa. xlix. 12).   It is evident [that Sinim means
China, and that the Toungoo mountains and
these Shan mountains, as well as the sea, are to
be made the Lord's way for introducing the gospel to the great empire of China.   Hitherto
Sinim has been reached only by the sea, and a
few fires have been kindled on the seashore.
When the Lord makes all these mountains a
way, and the approach from the west as well as
from the east and south, then the Celestial
Empire will hear the thunder of God's law 'all
around the heavens,' and the time of her redemp-
tion will be near.   Commercial enterprise is

urging its way through Burmah and the Shan
States, to get hold of the wealth of Western
China. Various plans have been laid, roads
projected, exploring tours set on foot, all with
the conviction that China can be reached advan-
tageously from the west. Must it always be
true that the men of this world are wiser than
the children of light? Should we not be equally
anxious to carry the gospel to Western China?
And can we not make these Shan and Karen
mountains a way?"

Now a wide and effectual door is open to us.
Who of us will grasp the banner of our King,
and hasten to take the land in his name? Who
will carry on the charge till final victory is won,
unless the young people of America awake to
the responsibility that is resting upon them?
As I look upon the great work already accomplished by our missionary organization, I feel
that there is no more glorious occupation to be
found than that of carrying the refreshing waters
of life to those whose parched and thirsty lips
might never quaff them from other hands than
ours.

In October of 1865, my father wrote, "The
Missionary Union is abundantly worthy of all
the confidence and support it receives, and

vastly more ; for it is doing a great work, — a
work exceeding, in the grandeur of its propor-
tions and its far-reaching influence, the highest
conceptions of its warmest friends. Have the
friends of the Union ever considered in how
many dialects and with how many voices the
Union preaches the gospel every Sunday, and
perhaps every day in the year? In Burmah
alone, the Union preaches in at least twelve
dialects, and I dare say the whole number ex-
ceeds twenty. Take into account also the
numerous preachers that speak in these various
dialects, including the printed pages that pro-
claim the way of life, and the Union's gospel
heralds would be numbered by hundreds and
thousands.

"If a preacher were found who could use
freely twenty different languages, and whose
heart burned within him to preach the gospel in
those languages, and only asked to be fed and
clothed and transported from place to place that
he might do so, who would not feel that it was
very important to give him an ample support ?
Who would not covet the privilege of giving
something to help him in the good work ?
Such a preacher is the Missionary Union. If
an angel were to fly in the visible heavens with

the everlasting gospel, proclaiming the way of life in a score of languages and with a thousand voices, who would not say, 'God speed thee in thy glorious flight!' Who would not be willing to give him wings? Such an angel is the Missionary Union. These languages and voices are being multiplied, — the fame and influence of this many-tongued preacher are annually widening. Let contributions also be multiplied, and let the resources of the Union be commensurate with the importance and grandeur of its work! God grant it, for Christ's sake!"

CHAPTER XII.

LAST DAYS IN BURMAH. — RETURN TO AMERICA. — MIS-
SIONARIES' CHILDREN.

WHILE on this journey my father became
very ill, and we were obliged to turn our faces
homewards.   The long journey over mountains
and through narrow passes was wearisome even
for a well person ; but for an invalid, unable to
partake of any nourishment except a little rice-
water, and scarcely able to sit upon his pony, it
was exceedingly difficult.   Our spirits lost their
buoyancy, and we failed to mark the beauty by
the way.   We were filled with the one idea of
reaching home in safety, which our kind heavenly Father permitted us to do.

Sad were the days that followed our return.
Several of the native disciples were ill.   Sickness entered our school and family, and my darling brother Willie died.   My father's illness
increased, and the physician said he must leave
the country.   My parents' hearts had long quiv-
ered with the thought that I must soon be sent

to America; and now, if my father must go, it would be the most favorable opportunity for me, so much better than to go with strangers. We hastily made arrangements to go to Rangoon. As the physician's verdict there was the same as in Toungoo, there was no alternative but to sail for America as soon as possible.

Bitter tears fell as swift fingers fashioned the garments needed for the voyage. Anguished hearts made earnest supplication to the ever-present Friend, who alone can sustain in the hour of trial.

But why linger upon these painful scenes? The last hour came, the good-bys were said, and from the deck of the ship we watched the little boat that carried back to shore mother and aunt and brother. They returned to carry on the work: we turned our faces towards the trackless ocean.

Shut up as I had been to the plain dwellings of the missionaries and the rude huts of the natives, the steamer seemed to me fit for a palace, and the broad ocean and blue sky filled my soul with a sense of ever-varying beauty. I rejoiced in the grandeur of the storm encountered in the Indian Ocean, the sight of the canal then in process of construction at Suez, and the

glimpse at the Pyramids, and the marble
mosques of Cairo. I was amused with the don-
keys and their drivers at Alexandria, and delighted with our short pause at Messina, with
the view of the coast of Sicily, and Mount
Etna, and Stromboli then smoking from its pent-
up fires ; with our passage between Scylla and
Charybdis, and our glimpse at the home of
Garibaldi.

Another storm met us in the Mediterranean,
but we arrived safely at Marseilles.

I cannot describe the emotions with which I
gazed upon the peculiarities of civilized lands,
in France and England : the people everywhere
wearing full suits of clothes, the good roads,
the convenient, elegant carriages, the beautiful
homes, the magnificent public buildings, and
landscapes cultivated as far as the eye could
reach. As I think of them now, I recall the
question of another little child, not a missionary's, "Is it dark in the country where you
lived?" and I answer her, "Yes, little one,
dark, — not for want of sunlight, but for want
of heart-light."

The broad Atlantic seemed but a little step
between us and America. The Fourth of July
saw us in New York, and the next day we were

among dear friends. The fairy-like land of America, with its schools, its churches, and many wonders, was at last a reality to the missionary child ; and she felt, among its throngs of people, like a grain of sand on the seashore.

The reader here may pause, and say, "I do not find much 'child-life' in this book." True. A missionary's child has very little real child-life. People in this country can hardly understand how peculiar the life of a missionary's child is. It is begun with enfeebled physical conditions. The first few years are spent in the midst of heathenism. His playmates, if any, are native children. He has none of the opportunities of a Christian land. He has no instruction but that which his parents, already overburdened with work, can give; and the shadow of the coming separation hangs over every day's experience. When the time is fixed, who can describe the emotions of the weeks that follow? the dread, the fear, the heart-rebellings of the child; the scalding tears, the prayers, the heart-breaking struggles of the parents. Then comes the hour of parting. The last loving words are said, the last embrace is given, the last united petition laid before the throne of a covenant-keeping God, and the ves-

sel sails.   In vain do the children lean over the
vessel's side, and cry, "Speak to me once more:"
only the waves reply.

Mothers, can you form any idea of the anguish
of those loving hearts, and of the strange deso-
lation of the child?   Do you sympathize with
them as they bear this trial "for Jesus' sake"?

Through the dreary weeks that follow, in the
midst of storms and sea-sickness and exhaus-
tion, in perils by sea and perils by land, how the
heart yearns for the soothing presence and tender hand of the mother, and for the strong, loving protection of the father!   But the journey
ends ; and the missionary child treads upon the
soil so dear to his parents, but so new and
strange to him.

Here he occupies an anomalous position.

Children in this country are often compelled
by circumstances to go from home to obtain
their education, or enter upon other pursuits ;
but they carry with them sweet remembrances
of a home to which they may return in the hour
of need, and find a glad welcome.   It takes but
a few days, at most, for them to return.

But the missionary's child is a stranger in a
strange land.   Oceans and continents lie between him and his home ; weeks or months

must pass before even a letter can reach him. Too often his sore heart is wounded by comments upon his outlandish, unfashionable appearance. Too often he is caressed and even flattered, not for his own, but his parents' sake. Questions, too, are asked which pierce his heart. New scenes and untried paths are before him, which he must meet and pass alone. In health, in sickness, and in death, he is peculiarly alone.

These are some of the trials of missionaries' children; but there are compensations also. The Lord of hosts has not forsaken them, the God of Jacob is still their refuge. The earnest prayers of the parents, who thus sacrifice their all for Christ's sake, are not unheard. They reach the ear of the Father, "who so loved the world that he gave his only begotten Son," to endure sorrow and shame such as mortal has never known, that he might redeem the world unto himself. *His* heart beats in tender symprthy with the torn and bleeding hearts of the parents, who thus, in their part, "fill up the measure of Christ's sufferings." He heals their wounds, and strengthens their faith. He cares for their children, I believe, with a peculiar tenderness. He calls them all "by name," and hides them in the secret of his pavilion. He makes the crooked places straight, and the rough places smooth, before them. He gives them friends and educational advantages. '

It is now nearly seventy years since our missions began ; and the children of our missionaries are scattered in various parts of our country, and are engaged in every variety of honorable pursuit. At least twenty-five have returned to the mission-field. Others are studying with that in view.

Many have fallen victims to the climate, and are buried on mission ground. There is scarcely a missionary mother who cannot count one or more little graves. The first Christian grave at Bahmo was that of a missionary's child. In Burmah alone, we can count at least fifty little ones who have died. " Little Maria sleeps by the side of her mother." Many are buried side by side with native Christians ; some are sleeping in the solitary wilds of the jungle, with nought but the waving branches of the bamboo to mark their resting-place.

Which is the more bitter cup, to lay the loved one in his last little bed, when we know he is safe in the arms of Jesus ; or to send him home to a strange land, where he must bear temptations and trials without a parent's guiding hand ?

"In Ramah was there a voice heard, lamenta-
tion and weeping and great mourning; Rachel
weeping for her children, and would not be comforted, because they are not." In Ramah, not
in Burmah. The missionary mother utters no
complaint when her loved ones are taken. She
turns to her labor for others, and "the days go
on."

But the thought of sending her little ones
home weighs like a heavy burden upon her
heart. How shall the children be provided for
in a distant land? is the question which constantly returns. In the past, many precious
homes have been opened to these children, and
friends have kindly given them a place among
their own. But sometimes parents have been
obliged to return to the field, leaving their children without a settled home; though this may
now be avoided by the opportunities of the
"Home for Missionaries' Children," recently
opened. It is the outgrowth of the motherly
sympathies of the Woman's Foreign Missionary
Society; and may the blessing of God rest upon
it!

In addition to the unavoidable anguish, missionaries are often compelled, on leaving their
children, to contend with bitter opposition on

the part of those who should be their sympa-
thizers and friends.   Reproaches are heaped
upon them, which render their heavy burden
almost unbearable.   Oh, rather, let every Christian worker feel the tenderest sympathy for
these parents, help them by their prayers, and
do all in their power to render the lives of missionary children happy and successful!